BOOK REVIEWS

"This is the second book in the series. A modern retelling of Beauty and the Beast, this story is filled with mystery, intrigue, action and adventure. Ms. Archer did a wonderful job of developing the characters into strong, likable people. I really liked the characters Bella and Jack. Bella is a strong and willful girl. Jack is the wounded hero - demanding but full of love. They come together in a marriage of convenience but get out of it so much more than they bargained for. This is a beautifully written story with emotion and depth and it was a delight to read." ~BookBub Reviewer

"I am loving this family and this series. The suspense is great and makes it interesting. The characters are amazing." ~ Amazon Reviewer

THE BILLIONAIRE'S MARRIAGE CONTRACT

MELODY ARCHER

WANT MORE SWEET ROMANCE?

Eliza and Daniel Stevenson's Love Story is *waiting for you to enjoy!* **Simply, click the link below to grab your copy of this Free Sweet Romance :)**
Go here: www.memorablefictionbooks.com/pages/free-book

"True, that he's no Prince Charming but there's something in him that I simply didn't see." Bella

CHAPTER ONE

ack

"How can you ask me to marry again?" Jack Walker Stevenson knelt by his great-grandfather's grave in a quiet corner of Paradise Lake's cemetery.

His voice sounded raw to his own ears. "You always were a stubborn old coot. But, forcing me to marry by my twenty-seventh birthday to receive my inheritance is simply too much."

"Making that old silver mine my own is something I've wanted for years, but I can't let myself fall in love only to be rejected again. Don't you remember what happened with Elin?"

Memories haunted him of the woman he'd married

during his wild college days. Elin had been beautiful and full of life.

After a whirlwind romance, they flew to Las Vegas and eloped. Jack had been convinced she loved him as much as he loved her. Only six months into their marriage and he had discovered just how fickle his new wife's love really was.

Jack hadn't realized how obsessed Elin was about appearances, or more specifically how he appeared to her friends. Her image was something his wife fixated on relentlessly.

Which was why she used him to fix her image. She had used him to pay off her gambling debts.

She'd even refused to discuss the idea of children with him. Her youth -- her beauty that she'd known would be fleeting -- she'd tried to hold onto with a fierce grip. She'd held onto it at any cost.

These were things he had found out after they were married.

After she lied to him, Jack lost a lot of trust but he'd wanted to do whatever it took to make their marriage work especially after he found out she was pregnant.

Jack's brows puckered as he remembered what had been the final straw. It was why his wife had left him.

He'd been at a science fair and had chased down a thug to save a teenager from a kidnapping and whatever horrible fate waited her. He traced a finger down the scar on his right cheek — a reward for his efforts.

Jack could still picture the look of revulsion on Elin's face when the stitches came out.

Her words haunted him still. *I can't see this day after day*

Jack. I mean before you looked sort of like a rugged modern-day Tarzan, which I liked. But now, you look awful. You look horrible. You look beastly. I just can't be with you... not now.

The next day, she had left a handwritten note on the kitchen counter to let him know she was leaving. His wife had been seven months pregnant at the time. The police called him late the next night to tell him his wife had been hit by another vehicle and died instantly.

As had their unborn son.

Jack turned his head and caught sight of the tiny grave in the Stevenson family plot.

His gut clenched in tight knots. There was too much loss. Too much emptiness. Too much pain.

Angrily he wiped away a lone tear that slipped down his cheek.

Dark clouds hovered above the small town's skyline.

Thunder rumbled and raindrops splattered onto his face, following the length of his scar. The light raindrops were soothing. Cleansing the traces of wedged-in dirt that had been pressed into his palms.

His large Saint Bernard dog nudged his shoulder, licking his cheek. The roughness of his tongue, a healing salve against the pain.

Jack squatted and draped an arm around his furry companion, pulling him close.

Without warning a familiar voice interrupted the silence. "I saw today's date and thought I'd find you here."

Jack stood to his feet, turning as his brother approached him. "Yeah..."

Adam pulled Jack into a swift hug before standing at his side.

"Sorry it's a little rough for you this time of year."

Jack swung his gaze back to the graves in front of him. "Even though it's been four years, for some reason this year seems more difficult than usual." Jack rubbed a hand along the stubble of his chin, his voice low and gravelly. "I miss what could have been."

Adam didn't speak only nodded and listened. Jack was grateful for that. Somehow, his brother's presence offered more support than any words could.

Shifting his feet, Jack slipped his thumbs in the belt loops of his jeans. "With my twenty-seventh birthday just around the corner and Grand's will staring me in the face, I'll admit today has felt like a stomach punch."

"You don't have to follow through on Grand's Will requirements."

"I know." Jack sighed. "Problem is, I want Grand's silver mine way too much to pass it up. But, I also don't want to marry again which leaves me at an impasse."

Adam cocked his head to the side and looked at him. "Maybe you just need to do what I did and find a woman who will agree to marriage-in-name-only for a year."

"Hmm… maybe. Problem is, that whole not-falling-in-love idea backfired on you."

"True. But, I wouldn't trade marrying Elle for the world." Adam's contented look was as disturbing as it was annoying.

A quick surge of jealousy rose to the surface at his brother's happiness which he quickly tamped down. He was glad for Adam. He deserved happiness. But four years ago he believed that kind of happiness was possible for him too and that went horribly wrong. No, that kind of soul satisfying love wasn't gonna happen for him.

"I'm happy for you, I really am. But somehow I just don't see that happening for me."

"I think you might be surprised at how the right woman simply shows up when it's your turn for love Jack." The corner of Adam's lips turned up into a knowing smile.

His brother might have found the right woman, but it didn't seem possible for him. Jack needed some girl who wouldn't mind living in the mountains at least some of the time. She'd have to be part tomboy and part crazy to marry him.

Most of all he needed a woman who wouldn't run away as far and as fast as they could at the sight of his scar.

No, Jack couldn't see himself finding a woman to love anytime soon.

Love just wasn't possible, not for him.

A loud crack of thunder rang out above their heads and the sky opened up pouring down rain.

"That's our cue to head on home." Jack turned and whistled for his dog. "Brahms, here boy."

His large dog turned away from chasing some birds to run after Jack as he walked to his truck. Adam opened his truck door and stopped. "I'll pick up Elle and meet you at your place. The family's already there waiting to see you."

"All right." Jack sighed and opened the door. Brahms jumped in, skidding to the passenger seat on the other side. His dog shook his thick fur coat, spraying water all over Jack's face and arms.

He picked up the towel he kept in his truck and dried him off. As he drove out of their small town and up the back road that led to his mountain home, he exhaled a slow breath as he thought of his loving and protective family.

They had decided to show up today because they didn't want him to have to go through this difficult day alone.

As grateful as he was for his family's love and concern, Jack found it somewhat annoying that he needed them. His pride bristled that after four years, this day still crippled him emotionally.

It frustrated Jack that he was so predictable. That he needed his family's support on this day every year.

Driving up the gravel road, a glimpse of his massive twelve-bedroom log home at the top of the hill, was like a homing beacon to him.

The large twenty thousand square foot house was built on top of a mountain, twenty miles away from the nearest town.

Here he was far away from critical eyes. Here he was far away from sharp tongues. Here he was far away from the possibility of anyone poking at the walls around his bruised heart.

For Jack, this was his safe zone.

Which was why he had made the house so huge in the first place. He used the entire west wing for himself. He built this house as a private oasis which included a spacious bedroom, a large office, a few guest bedrooms, library, media room, gym and swimming pool.

He stopped at the iron gate, punched in the security

code and drove through to his six car garage. Another click of the button opened the garage door.

Only his family knew the security code.

"Brahms, come here boy." He whistled for his dog whose massive body pounded toward him. "It's time for your shower." Jack had installed a small dog shower when he had the house built. It was made for days like this when it rained, so his dog wouldn't track dirt or mud all over the house.

Grabbing the towel he started to dry off his dog, but Brahms was too quick.

"I've got him sir." Benedict Coggins picked up the towel and held Brahms by his collar. As usual his resolute personal assistant was right where he needed him. He'd been running this house since Jack designed and built it three years ago.

Jack realized how dependent he was on Ben. It wasn't something he liked to see in himself, but he was grateful for Ben's help.

"Thanks Ben."

"Your family is in the great room, sir. Mrs. Potter has already served snacks and set the rest of the food and drinks on the large kitchen table." Ben finished drying off his dog and Brahms ran off down the hall. "Is there anything else you need?"

"Not right now. Thank you Ben."

"Very good sir." Ben nodded once before hurrying to his next task.

Jack walked down the hall to the great room. The home's structure had allowed for a vast open expanse twenty feet high with beams that stretched floor to ceiling.

The arching pillars and open space had reminded Jack of a Cathedral's ability to capture Heaven. Its towering expanse cried security and sanctuary.

Walking past the open French doors that led to the Conservatory, he inhaled the sweet scent of roses that permeated the hallway. He planned to cut a rose for his mom and Elle before they left for home.

The sun shone through the kitchen and dining room spreading cheer throughout the house.

As he entered the dining area he walked past his cook, Mrs. Potter and her grandson Chipper, carrying pans of finger sandwiches, muffins and other goodies to the large dining table and side table.

"Just let me know if there's anything else you need, Mr. Stevenson."

"Smells good. Thanks Mrs. Potter and Chipper." Jack nodded at them as they hurried back into the kitchen.

He turned and walked toward his family, seated at the kitchen counter and table talking with one another.

"Jack, you're here. Good." His mother saw him first and slid off the stool where she sat by the kitchen counter. She walked over to him giving him one of her comforting hugs.

"Ah, mom." He wrapped his arms around her holding her close, taking in a moment of child-like serenity. "You didn't have to drive all the way here today."

"We wanted to be here for you. Family sticks together." The slight shimmer of moisture in his mom's eyes told him how important he was to her.

"Thank you. I appreciate it." He could always count on his mom to be there for him. That was something for which he was very grateful.

"You doing okay Jack?" Eliza Stevenson persisted. It hadn't changed much since he was a young boy until now. He knew his mom well enough to know she would continue to ask questions until she was satisfied.

"It was a tougher day, but I'm doing good. It helps to be with family." Jack kissed his mom's cheek happy when the shimmer of tears was replaced with a big smile.

"Good."

"Hey Jack." Gabe called from where he sipped a cup of coffee, leaning a hip against the kitchen island. Behind him sat Luke and Zach who nodded and went back to their deep discussion.

"Don't you guys have anything better to do on a Saturday?" He forced himself into a lighter mood as he gave them each a fist bump.

"Apparently not. For some reason we care more about you than the latest Seahawks game." Gabe shot him a grin.

Jack walked over to the coffee maker and started measuring out the coffee grounds to make another pot of coffee. "You didn't have to take time out of your busy schedule to show up here today." Jack knew his brother. Usually Gabe's life was so well organized that he didn't go out of his way unless it was important.

"I wanted to. You're my brother and I care about you. So, how has it really been going today?" His brother's bright blue eyes seemed to see through him like a targeted laser beam.

He was annoyed that his brother understood him so

well. It's also probably what made Gabe so good at all that personal development stuff he did.

Jack rubbed the back of his neck. "To answer your question, I've done a lot of thinking today. Not much of it was good." Jack grabbed a coffee cup and poured the hot brown liquid near to the brim. Lifting it he took a sip, peering over the rim at his brother.

"That's what I thought." Gabe finished drinking his coffee, and set the mug in the sink. "We're here for you, man. Anytime you want to talk."

Suddenly the door opened and Adam walked inside with his very pregnant wife at his side.

"Adam, are you sure you should be bringing your lovely wife anywhere at this late date?" Jack kissed his sister-in-law on the cheek. He did his best not to let any worries show.

"You try telling my wife anything. She makes up her own mind. And I don't relish the thought of sleeping on the couch." Adam slapped him on the back.

"Jack, I'll be fine. You and Adam both worry too much." Elle waddled over to the fridge and poured herself an orange juice.

Carrying the cool drink, Elle walked over to the picture that sat on the fireplace mantle.

It was a photo of Jack and Elin. She had been four months pregnant at the time. A friend had taken that picture on his smartphone, because Jack wanted to record every detail to show his son when he was older. Sadly, that wasn't to be.

"Do you still miss them, Jack?"

"I miss what could have been." Jack sighed, wondering

how Elle managed to always get him to answer her probing questions.

"Well, I think that's normal after four years."

"Maybe." Jack didn't want things to be normal. He wanted to stop feeling the pain of his loss and loneliness. Still, he was glad his mom and grandparents didn't know all the details of what happened those last few days before his wife and unborn child died. Perhaps someday he'd tell them what really happened.

Elle walked over to sit on a chair next to her husband, her hand toying with Adam's.

"Do you still want the inheritance Grand left you?" Adam sipped on his coffee, peering up at him over the rim.

"Yeah. Just one problem. There's no girlfriend." Jack shrugged half-heartedly and slipped his hands in his pockets.

"Well, about that." Elle looked at her husband who nodded before her gaze moved back to Jack. "I thought maybe it would be a good idea to invite guests to a private dinner right here. It might help move things along."

Things. She meant it would help get his life moving along.

Jack couldn't fault her for trying. He'd spent a lot of years just getting by in this cave-like existence. He'd found a comfortable rhythm here which was why he pushed back against change.

"I don't think I want to know." Jack sighed knowing Elle would tell him the details anyway.

"I know, but we want to help." Elle took a sip of her orange juice and began. "We were thinking of inviting some of my friends and some people both you and Adam know. We made a list."

"I hate schmoozing. Heck, I don't even get out much except once a week to go to the office and the occasional benefit gala." Jack flicked away a stray piece of lint on his sleeve with impatience. "If I need to network with people, I invite them here to my own turf."

"I know but this is important Jack."

Jack realized his sister-in-law would keep pestering him until he gave in. He didn't want to meet people. He didn't want to get close to others. He didn't want to feel that kind of pain again. But maybe, if he did this then Elle would get off his back about trying to set him up.

"All right. Let's see it." Jack could feel the pulse at the base of his throat as he grabbed the list. His finger slowly trailed down the list of names, some of whom he recognized.

"You'll see three friends of mine that you haven't met, on that list."

Jack groaned inwardly. "Since they're your friends, go ahead and invite them." Jack inhaled a deep breath and blew it out slowly. "I'll meet them but I can't make any promises that it'll go any further."

"I understand." Elle's gaze burned into his. "Does that mean you're okay with me sending these invitations?"

He nodded once. "You organize everything and I'll be here." Jack surprised himself as the words flew from his lips. He grimaced.

He was not looking forward to this.

"Good." Elle looked up, a pink glow on her cheeks and a large grin on her face. "Let's plan this dinner so it will happen in two weeks. I'll talk to your event coordinator Maisie Merriweather and we'll get these sent out quickly. That will give everyone enough time to rearrange their calendars. I'll invite some of Adam's and your friends too, Jack." Elle took out her smartphone and started typing notes.

Jack agreed to the extra invitations, but the reason was to make Elle happy more than anything else. He didn't have high expectations of meeting a woman whom he would want to marry.

One thing was for sure, he would be relieved when this dinner was over and done with.

"I HOPE you're ready to go to battle with the wolves to get what you want Jack." Alex one of his associate Architects, eyed him and grabbed a drink from a waiter who made his way through the maze of people.

"I'm ready." Jack walked over to welcome the members of Paradise Lake land development office. He hated schmoozing at these events, but it needed to be done so he could get the go-ahead for the Adventure Park his team was designing.

"Mayor Rainey, glad you could meet with us today to discuss plans."

"Well Jack, your idea intrigued me. But, don't get too hopeful. You need to convince us first." Leah Rainey, looked around the room at the men and women who stood by her side, each one nodding their agreement. She was surrounded by her yes men and women.

"I figured there would need to be some discussion and that's why we're here." Jack was confident that the Paradise Lake planning council would soon see that his proposal was as good for the town as it was for him. "If you'll all follow me to the large media room we can begin."

"This ought to be good." Bert Wolffe snorted and looked at his brother Bart who shook his head and chuckled. They were Mayor Rainey's closest advisors and open opponents to Jack's planned development.

Jack led everyone into the large media room that was located just off the great room. He had this room built just in case he needed a large conference room for group meetings.

Mrs. Potter stood there organizing the coffee and snacks on the side table. She nodded to Jack and hurried out of the room. Ben followed her and closed the double doors behind him.

"Help yourself to coffee or tea, find a spot at the table and we'll start the presentation shortly." Jack motioned to the massive boardroom table that seated thirty people.

With a press of a button a panel slid up to the ceiling, revealing a white screen. Jack opened the laptop and located the slides for his presentation.

Opening his mouth to speak, Jack paused. Dunlin Campbell, his creative works project manager walked in with his samples.

"Jack, here are the newest design mock-ups you asked for." Dunlin handed him a bunch of samples of the ideas they came up with.

"Thanks Dunlin. Looks like everything is good to go. Alex?"

Alex stood to her feet and welcomed everyone to the meeting. Jack had hired her to be the face of Stevenson Creative Works, since his own face seemed to repel most people. Normally he didn't show up for these meetings, but this was his passion project. He needed to be here.

"And now, Jack Stevenson will share his vision for this project." Alex's gaze moved to Jack and he stood to his feet walking to the front of the room.

"The *Rose Adventure Park* was inspired by a few people in my life. One of them was my own mother whose childhood was filled with abuse and neglect. I wanted to find a way to bring a little happiness back into the lives of children. That's how the idea for this theme park was born." Jack slowly scrolled through the slides showing their designs of fun and unique rides for children.

"A favorite ride of mine is the pirate ship that floats on a river of water and encircles the enchanted castle. The ship runs on underwater cables, so the children are safe. The ship also sails under the castle where the children get to see and explore hidden treasure." Jack pointed out the castle and the water moat located in the centre of the adventure park that has many different rides, restaurants and stores for kids on the outskirts of the adventure park.

"These are well thought out designs for this adventure park. My question is, why should the Paradise Lake town council approve these changes to land development? What possible benefit would this bring to our peaceful town?" Mayor Rainey eyed Jack pointedly, sipping her coffee as she waited for his answer.

Bart Wolffe, one of the Mayor's henchmen spoke up.

"It looks to me like this development idea would only bring unnecessary traffic and noise to our peaceful town."

"It's important to consider all aspects of a project to make a good decision, don't you think?" Jack studied the group around the table.

"Of course." Mayor Rainey spoke up.

Jack continued. "Then we'd do well to consider the positive aspects. All this traffic would mean many parents and grandparents would bring their children to Paradise Lake. Which means, the town would receive a lot of additional income from tourists who drive through. I would venture to say, that new businesses would be created just because of the Adventure Park."

Jack took a breath and hit home the point that he knew would pique the Mayor's interest. "This Adventure Park would also make our small town more visible in this state and across the nation. I believe there would be many new opportunities to connect with other mayors and Government officials of different states."

"Hmm. I do like that idea." The corners of Mayor Rainey's mouth turned up and the star-gazed look in her eyes told Jack she was dreaming of all the possibilities.

Jack knew the mayor was interested in influence and power, which was why he wanted to end his presentation at this point. They needed to have a few days to think about the possibilities.

"This is a good place to table this discussion and give everyone here more time to consider this proposal from all angles."

"Yes, that's a good idea." The Mayor stood up and

shook his hand. "Thanks Jack. You've given us a lot to think about."

The Wolffe brothers stood beside the Mayor and stared at Jack, the scowls on their faces reminding him of circling predators.

"You're welcome. And please take mock-ups of the project designs back to the town office to give you a better idea of what we discussed here today."

Dunlin carried the mock-ups over and gave them to the Mayor's assistant.

Coggins saw to it that the Mayor and her team were escorted to the door. Soon they drove off Jack's driveway and down the hill.

Jack walked with Dunlin out the front door, eager to hear his thoughts. "What do you think? Will the Mayor accept our proposal?"

"I think the lassie would be crazy not to accept it. But, those two wolves who are circling her and us, might mean the difference between whether we have a long or short battle on our hands."

"Yeah I was thinking the same thing." Jack rubbed his bearded chin thoughtfully. He opened the door. "We'll talk about it next... week."

Jack stood there a moment stuttering to finish his sentence.

Bella, Dunlin's daughter walked up to him. Big brown eyes looked up into his own. Her heart shaped face was framed by brown hair that highlighted creamy smooth skin.

Her cheeks flushed as she looked at him.

"Hi Bella." Jack remembered the last time he'd seen her

had been at Adam's wedding. To his way of thinking, she was more beautiful now than she'd been back then. He also remembered that Bella had been one of those rare women who didn't even notice his scar.

"Hi, Mr. Stevenson." When she spoke his name in her light sing song voice, Jack felt himself drawn even more to her.

Meanwhile Jack kept his gaze on Dunlin's daughter. "It's been awhile. I hear you've been in college studying design."

"Yes, I've enjoyed it. Just finished my final exams actually." She pushed back a stray tendril of hair that snuck its way out of her hair clip.

He watched as Bella's father walked to the waiting car and set his things inside.

Before he could stop himself, Jack blurted. "You could come work here with your Dad in the Creative Design department."

"As much as I appreciate your offer Mr. Stevenson, I have a couple of job offers I'm looking at." Bella's polite refusal surprised and irked him. How could she say no to his offer? Her Dad worked for him for years. Did she know what she was giving up?

And yet, his pride aside, her confident independence sparked an ember of admiration for her.

"I'd encourage you to take a look at what we offer here Bella. The position won't be open indefinitely."

"I understand Mr. Stevenson. My answer is the same."

Jack nodded and saw that Bella's cheeks had turned a deep pink color. "Well if you change your mind, I'll give you my number to text or call."

"I'm sure that won't be…"

"Here's my personal number." Jack interrupted her and stepped closer handing her his card and speaking the number in her ear. Breathing deeply, he could smell a delightful mixture of garden and books. It was a heady combination.

"Got it. Thanks, Mr. Stevenson." Bella stepped away from him her cheeks redder then before if that were possible.

He reached for her hand. "And Bella?"

She peered up at him a new wariness in her big beautiful eyes.

"It's not Mr. Stevenson. Call me Jack."

"I don't think that's a good idea." Bella objected. Jack could almost hear the argument in her head that he was her Dad's boss. In some ways Bella was a woman who liked to do things properly. She wouldn't like the idea of being too familiar with him.

"You might not think it's a good idea, but I do. I'd like you to call me by my name."

Bella folded her arms across her chest and narrowed her gaze.

"Okay then, Jack."

Large brown eyes looked up into his filled with spark and fire. That flash of something ignited a deeper attraction. He didn't know how long he stood still, mesmerized by her.

"My Dad's waiting for me. Goodbye Jack."

He nodded abruptly, angry with himself for letting a beautiful face turn his head.

Walking back inside the house, Jack closed the door and sighed.

He was frustrated for letting down the carefully constructed walls around his heart, if only for a moment. What was he doing offering Bella a job and giving her his personal number? What was wrong with him?

One thing was for sure, she stirred something in him that he wasn't ready for. Something he might never be ready for.

He needed to stay as far away from Bella as possible.

<h1 style="text-align:center">CHAPTER TWO</h1>

ella

BELLA BLINKED OWLISHLY at the early morning sun streaming through the window.

With slow movements, she made her way into the kitchen and set the coffee pot on the old cookstove.

Rubbing her eyes, she remembered the reason for her sleepless night.

Jack Stevenson.

Opening the blinds to the large kitchen window, she tried to get rid of the image of his handsome face and his muscled body.

His hazel eyes had held her captive, something which she sensed was commonplace for him.

Memories of the few times she'd seen Jack came back to her.

He'd saved her as a teenager at a science fair. Jack had chased down the thug that had dragged her into a dark alley, only to be attacked.

Shuddering, she remembered the blood that flowed from his cheek as he carried her to safety.

She'd given him the only thing she kept with her to wipe away the blood. Her mother's handkerchief. After she'd thanked him, he'd hurried away.

The next time she saw him had been last year at her best friend Elle's wedding. Jack's older brother Adam had married her best friend, so it was inevitable that they would see each other.

Jack still had the scar on his face, but his cynical side hadn't changed any.

He was still pushy and demanding.

Yet despite all of that, she found him attractive even though she desperately didn't want to. She chalked it up to a childhood admiration for his heroic act in saving her life.

"Is that coffee I smell?" The back door to the kitchen opened and her dad's slow footsteps fell along the cold hard wood floor.

He sat down at the kitchen table with a heavy sigh. Bella reached up into the cupboard and brought down his favorite coffee cup. Pouring the steaming brew into his mug, she set it in front of him.

Bella sat down beside him and frowned. "Are you feeling okay today Dad?"

"Aye, sure I am Beauty." Dunlin Campbell reverted back to the Scottish brogue from his childhood whenever he was tired or upset about something. "*Whist,* are you worried?"

"I always worry about you, you know that." Bella reached over and squeezed his hand calloused from all the hours he spent working on inventions. It was because her dad had invented some household items that Jack had first connected with him.

A few years ago, Jack had started an online members only website for scientists and inventors and her dad had joined. Her dad's inventions had been featured a few times. They continued to get to know each other and that's why they decided to meet at the science fair years ago.

When Jack hired her dad as his creative projects manager years ago, her father had finally been able to have a steady income and was able to set a little money aside to help her go to college.

She was grateful for that, but now she wondered if all the responsibilities her dad took on weren't too much for him.

As Bella sipped her coffee, she spotted the dark circles under his eyes.

"I know, but I wish you wouldn't. Besides I'm fine." Her dad drank his coffee his blue-grey eyes boring holes into hers. "If anyone should be worried, it's me."

"Why's that?"

"Yesterday, you actually turned down a great job offer from Jack Stevenson. Lassie, why would you do such a thing?"

Bella squirmed under her dad's probing gaze. She'd hoped to avoid this conversation. "Listen Dad. I know you have a great job with Jack that comes with great pay and benefits, but I just don't think it's a good idea for us both to work there."

"Why ever not?" Her dad set down his coffee cup and leaned closer. "Jack knows he can expect me and you, to be professional in our work. It wouldn't hinder his business, it would only make it better."

Bella put her hand on her dad's arm, her way of calming him down and helping him to really listen to her. "I know we would work well together, but right now I want the freedom to make my own way. I want to have the confidence that comes from being independent and getting started on my own."

"I suppose I understand that even though I really wish you would work with me. I could see you taking over my job and being great at it."

"Thanks for the vote of confidence, but I'm not so sure about that. Anyway that's not…" Her dad interrupted.

"I know, that's not what you want." Her dad sighed, a crooked smile his show of surrender. "Well, you know I'll support you in whatever you decide."

"Thanks Dad. You're the best."

"So I've been told." He winked at her.

A sudden knock at the door interrupted their morning coffee.

"That'll be Rory. She was going to pick me up today." Bella got up and put her cup by the sink before she opened the door. "Come in Rory. I'll just get my jacket."

Her friend talked with her dad for a minute while Bella slipped on her jacket. Bella walked to the door and turned.

"I only work a half day today so I should be home early afternoon, okay?"

"Sure." Her dad called out, but Bella could tell his mind was already on a new project. Today was Saturday, which was the day he used to work on his latest invention. Knowing her dad, he would be so busy on his new project, that he wouldn't even notice she was gone.

Bella hurried out the door with Rory to the waiting car. She took turns with her friends driving to work. Since Bella and her Dad shared their only truck, they had figured out a plan.

Bella hadn't needed a vehicle in college because she was able to walk everywhere. But now that she had finished college, she needed to save her money to buy a used car.

As she opened the door to the car, she saw Rory's three aunts smiling in the back seat.

"Hello, Aunt Florrie, Aunt Fawn and Aunt Merrie."

"Bella dear. It's lovely to see you again." Aunt Merrie was the most talkative of Rory's three aunts. "Don't mind us, dearie. We're just along for the ride."

"Every two weeks we come to Paradise Lake to get groceries and supplies." Rory looked at Bella meaningfully.

"Of course." Bella knew Rory's three aunts were very insistent that they knew where Rory was at all times. Rory had mentioned that her Aunt Mal was quite bitter over a family feud from years ago and at one point had threatened Rory. So the three aunts never let Rory out of their sight.

"But today I'm excited to do some research for my next romance novel." Rory threw her a wide smile.

Bella was always amazed at how her friend enjoyed the simple pleasures, even though her life was very confining. Maybe that's why she had such a good imagination and was such a great author.

"What's your newest romance about?"

"A poor girl who unexpectedly meets a Prince and they fall in love." Rory shrugged. "Hey, what can I say? I love sappy romance stories."

Rory parked in the space behind the Library building. They all got out of the car and headed towards the Library. Bella and Rory walked side by side, talking.

Bella reached over and picked up her friends hand, squeezing it gently. In the past few years, she had grown closer to Rory, seeing her regularly at the Library. It was always good to see her friend. Yet, Bella was grateful she didn't have those type of restrictions placed on her and hoped soon Rory would have more freedom too.

Rory sighed. "Anyway, how's it going finding a job?"

"Well, I have two interviews next week. But to my surprise, my Dad's boss offered me a job yesterday."

"Jack Stevenson?"

"Yeah. I said no. I just don't think it would be a good idea to work for the same guy that my Dad works for. Besides, I want to do more and see more than what I'm doing right now. Being stuck forever in the life I'm living right now is not what I want. Do you know what I mean?" Bella looked at the blue sky that hovered just above their small town.

"I understand that." Rory grimaced as she looked at her.

"Anyway, I'm rambling. We should probably get inside before Molly sends a search party." Bella opened the door and they walked together into the Paradise Lake Library. Rory walked toward the aisles that contained research books while Bella was cornered by the head Librarian.

"Bella, I'm so happy to see you back with us again even if it is only part-time." Molly wrapped big arms around Bella's shoulders and squeezed her in a tight embrace.

"I'm happy to be back, Molly."

"Well now that you're back, I have a couple of things for you to do. I know you've been studying creative design, so I was hoping you could take a look at our Library's website this morning. Then in a couple hours, I have a young girl that I'd like you to work with who is struggling with reading. I know how good you are with the children Bella, so I saved that task for you."

"Two of my favorite things to do. Sounds great." Bella followed Molly to her corner office where the Librarian gave her the login information for the website.

After a couple of hours, Bella had completed the updates and redesign of the front pages of the website.

"It's done." Bella walked over to where Molly worked.

Molly brought the Library's website up onto her browser window and gushed over the new design changes. "Bella, this is beautiful. The teal and yellow colors with a few splashes of red, make the Library fun and appealing to the young people. Thank you!"

"I'm happy to help."

"Now I'll be able to tell Vonda at the town office that

our Library website no longer gives our small town a bad reputation. She'll most likely ask you to redesign the town office website. Which is horribly out dated by the way, but don't tell her I said so." Molly gave a cheeky grin. "Now, I want to introduce you to a beautiful young girl who needs your help."

Bella grinned inside at how competitive Molly was with the other offices in town. The town Librarian was an unpredictable mixture of fun and sassy, which she kind of liked.

She followed Molly to the children's section of the Library where they found a dozen young children, busy turning the pages of picture books.

"Angel, I have someone I'd like you to meet." Molly spoke quietly to a young girl who looked to be around eight years old. The little girl stood to her feet and pushed back brown hair that hung in strands by her face. Slowly, she peered up at Bella.

Bella crouched down so she could see Angel's eyes. "I'm Bella, Angel. Nice to meet you. Do you like stories?"

"Yeth." She lisped and played with the end of one of her thick braids.

"Me too. Could I read you a story today?"

The little girl nodded and ran over to the bookcase filled with children's books and pulled one off the shelf.

"Let's go outside and sit in the sun to read today okay?"

Angel slipped her hand in Bella's and they walked outside towards a bench shaded by a tall poplar tree.

The little girl curled up on the bench beside Bella as she started reading the story. She was about halfway through when suddenly they were interrupted.

"Bella Campbell. It's been too long since we last saw each other." Mason Rogers stood in front of her, his large shadow spilling over onto both of them. As usual her ex-boyfriend had his buddy following close behind. His constant sidekick from school had stuck around.

"Hi Mason."

"It's no surprise that we find you at the Library, isn't that right Chuck?" Mason elbowed his friend who only grunted a response.

"Hi Chuck it's good to see you." Bella was irritated that Chuck was once again being used by Mason as a pawn in his sordid mind games.

Chuck hung his head and whispered. "Hello Bella."

"What do you want Mason?" Bella didn't have time to play games. She'd finished dealing with Mason when they went their separate ways in High School and didn't want to begin again.

He had been the star of the football team and chose to spend his time making himself look good or adding another beautiful girl to a notch on his belt. Both of those things he'd done while he dated her.

It looked like Mason hadn't changed much after five years.

"Same thing I've always wanted… you darling." Mason put one hand behind her head and leaned in close to whisper. "You still look good. If you were beside me, you'd look even better. We always were the best looking couple around Bella."

She didn't know whether to laugh or cry out in indignation at his self-inflated words. Shifting on the bench she moved herself out of his reach. "Mason we might look good together, but you and me getting back together isn't going to happen."

"Bella you don't mean that. When you stop and remember how good it was between us, you'll agree with me." Mason put one foot on the bench and reached over to wrap his fingers around the ends of her hair. "So why don't you finish your little story-time with this child, then you can come ride around town with me in my new truck."

Pulling away she stood to her feet. "Maybe I didn't make myself clear Mason. I don't want to go on a date or riding in your truck with you or anywhere else. Now, Angel and I are going back into the Library to finish our story."

Bella reached for the little girls hand and they walked toward the Library doors.

Mason spoke in a loud voice behind her. "This isn't over Bella, not by a long shot."

As she opened the door, she heard Mason revving his truck engine loudly before squealing the tires and driving away. She couldn't believe that after all these years, he still hadn't grown up. He was still trying to impress her with his good looks and fast vehicles.

Mason still didn't realize that's not what impressed her. She'd rather have a man who helped others, than a man like Mason who only thought about himself.

A picture of Jack came to mind. Where had that come from? As quick as that thought entered her thoughts, she tamped it down.

Bella pushed all other thoughts aside as they walked into the peaceful surroundings of the Library.

She and Angel drifted over to a quiet spot in the children's corner and resumed reading the story, happy to get her mind off of troubling thoughts.

BY WEDNESDAY THE FOLLOWING WEEK, Bella had been to both interviews only to be turned down for both positions.

She came home, kicked her shoes off and with a heavy sigh walked to her office space. Plopping down her purse on the desk, she paced. Bella was determined she wouldn't let this set back defeat her.

Rubbing the back of her neck, she hoped to get rid of the stress-induced tightening of her muscles.

As she remembered the last few days, she realized it hadn't been only the interviews that had her tense. Yesterday, Mason had stopped by again to ask her to go to a movie with him. Once again, Bella had turned him down. His truck kicked up rocks as he drove away.

Bella didn't want to make him angry, but she also didn't want to date him. She hoped he would give up, but somehow she didn't think she'd seen the last of him.

Sighing once again, she turned on her computer. She needed to refocus on finding a job. Opening her browser window she searched for job openings in creative design.

She needed the work to pay off her school loans and she wanted the money to continue to grow her online business for old and rare print books and maps.

The corners of her lips turned up as she looked around the office at the book shelves stacked with old and rare books. Those books were something she loved searching for at garage sales, estate sales and auctions.

She had set up her website two years ago after she was inspired by one of her college professors who had been looking for a particular book for years with no success.

Bella had done some digging and had given the book to him as a gift after finishing his course. The happiness on his face was all the thanks she needed.

Turning back to the computer she looked for job openings, happily finding one. She quickly uploaded her resume, wrote a cover letter and emailed it hoping to get an interview.

Taking a few more minutes she went to her rare books website only to see that two more orders had come in for out of print books.

Searching her inventory, she realized she only had one of the books. Doing another search, she found the book for this customer located at an out-of-the-way small town in Europe. She emailed the customer back to let them know it would take a little longer for their book to arrive.

Soon Bella went to the kitchen to start supper. She had just finished cooking the chicken stir-fry when her dad came home from work.

Her dad's heavy footsteps lumbered through the door and he stopped to kiss her on the forehead. "Ah, lassie. Does my heart good to see you doing a wee bit of cooking. Reminds me of your Mama's wonderful meals, God rest her soul."

"I just hope it tastes half as good as hers." Bella thought of the woman who gave birth to her - the woman she never knew - as she scooped up the rice and chicken stir-fry onto plates.

Her mom died when she was born, and she never knew her growing up. All of her childhood memories had just been about her and her dad. But, her dad had told her throughout the years how kind and generous her mom was and that she was a good cook.

Knowing this, inspired Bella to be more like her mom.

After a short blessing for the meal, they started eating. "I didn't get either job. But, I saw a new position that was accepting applications that I'm interested in. I've sent in my resume."

"Maybe it's a sign you're to work for Jack." Her dad winked at her.

"Dad getting turned down for a job is not a sign." Bella huffed and took a sip of water. She was convinced it was only her father who saw it that way.

"This is as good as your Mom's." Her dad winked at her.

"Don't try to butter me up, it won't make me change my mind."

He grinned and continued eating while studying her for a moment. "Now that you've learned to cook and you've got your schooling done, I'm eager to see you find a man to marry. It'll be good when you settle down with a husband you love and have children of your own."

Bella nearly choked on her water. "Dad, you're jumping the gun a little aren't you? You might be ready, but I'm not."

"I suppose there's still time yet, lassie. But don't make me wait years, okay?"

Bella took another sip of water. She didn't even know how to talk to her dad when he spouted off nonsense about seeing her married quickly. It frustrated her a little, seeing as just days ago she told her dad she was eager to get started on her own and become more independent. Sometimes it felt like whatever she said went in one ear and out the other.

They had just finished their meal when the loud sound of tires crunching against rocks disrupted their peaceful meal.

Bella cleaned up the dishes and there was a knock at the door.

Her dad opened it. "Maisie, come on in. Do you want a wee spot of tea?"

"Dunlin, I can always count on you to help me catch my second wind. Tea is just what I need." Maisie caught sight of Bella filling the water kettle as she followed her dad to the kitchen table.

"Bella dear, you look beautiful as usual. Always good to see you."

Bella smiled to herself as she finished boiling the water. Maisie Merriweather was her Dad's younger sister. She also worked as Jack Stevenson's event coordinator and organized people in the office for him as well as at his home. Maisie worked with Jack from the beginning and knew him better than anyone with the exception of his own family.

"Good to see you too, Aunt Maisie." Bella set two cups of tea down in front of them.

"Maisie, what brings you by tonight?" Her dad, never one for beating around the bush, got straight to the point.

"You mean other than the fact that I wanted to stop in to visit with my own brother and niece?" Her dad just grinned at his sister and waited.

"Well, there was another reason."

"Thought so. What is it?"

"Jack wanted me to stop by." Maisie reached into her purse and pulled out two envelopes and handed one to each of them. "Jack wanted to give each of you invitations to a private dinner he's having at his place on Friday night."

Bella opened the envelope and saw her name in gold letters. "He's inviting us to have dinner at his home. I was under the impression that Jack invited people to his home only on rare occasions."

"Normally that is true. But, I guess Adam's wife Elle talked him into having some friends over."

Dunlin's gaze switched from Maisie back to his daughter. "Well then, we won't want to miss this rare moment right, Beauty?"

"Of course." Bella forced a smile, but her belly was a churning mess.

Being in the same room as Jack would be beyond difficult. If he tried to push her to work for him again, she would stand her ground and say no to any offer he might make.

Clenching her jaw, Bella determined she would need to be at the top of her game if she was going to face Jack one more time.

CHAPTER THREE

Jack

JACK RUBBED the light stubble on his jaw and silently observed the people gathered under his roof.

This dinner party had become more than he bargained for.

Many women dressed in glittering dresses floated between the men around the room.

Waiters carrying glasses filled with wine and lemon water, silently made their way around the room. There were so many people in one place. Already Jack looked forward to returning to his hermit lifestyle.

But, he'd agreed to host this dinner in his home. Jack reminded himself that he was doing this for Elle and to find the wife he needed to secure his inheritance from his great-grandfather.

He sauntered casually into the room and seeing his event coordinator walked in her direction. She'd organized this event for them and with twenty-five years experience was very good at it.

"You've outdone yourself as usual, Maisie."

Maisie turned, her shoulder length grey hair bouncing and her smile wide. "Jack good to see you. And thanks." She looked around for a moment before turning back to him. "You know I always love coordinating a Stevenson brothers event."

"You're definitely the best person to handle all this." Jack knew that was an understatement as Maisie had worked twenty years as a senior marketing advisor before starting her own business as an Event Planner.

"Thank you Jack, that means a lot coming from you." She smiled and touched his arm. "Looks like one of the staff is waving me over. See you later Jack." She winked at him before hurrying away.

Jack grinned at the whirlwind that was Maisie Merriweather.

He turned and grabbed a lemon water from a waiter's tray before walking toward his sister-in-law who was waving him over. Elle and Adam were in the middle of a group of people bantering back and forth.

Jack recognized his friends in the group. Andrew Westcott, Nick Stefanos and Brock Harris were all friends he knew from college. It was good to see them.

He relaxed just a little as he walked toward Andrew. "Hey man, glad you could come tonight."

"Thanks for the invitation. At first I wasn't sure I'd be able to make it, with all the changes happening at my father's company." Andrew sighed. "Dad's retiring so that's thrown a hitch in my own plans."

"Are you looking to take over the company now that your Dad's retiring?" Jack hadn't talked a lot with Andrew since college.

"Yes. At least that's my Dad's plan." Andrew had been a good friend. They had studied together and even had a few spontaneous ski trips together.

"I take it you'd rather be skiing?"

"You got it. But, at some point we must take care of family responsibilities. I guess my time has come." Andrew sighed heavily.

"You aren't alone in that my friend."

"Yeah, I heard about your great-grandfather's will. Better you than me. Good luck finding a wife." Andrew chuckled and grinned, which Jack found annoying.

"You can laugh now, but sooner or later it'll happen to you too, my friend."

"I choose later. Much, much later." Andrew raised his glass to Jack's.

Jack forced a smile and gulped back the rest of his drink. A friend began speaking with Andrew and Jack's brother tapped him on the shoulder. Jack turned to see Adam standing beside Senator Carver.

"Jack, look who I found eating up Mrs. Potter's pastries." Adam grinned.

"I couldn't resist. They're delicious."

Jack shook the Senator's hand. "I'll let her know, John. It's good to see you again. How are things going?"

"It's going good for the most part. Working on lowering taxes and creating more jobs just like I promised."

"Good, good. Your family's well?" Both Jack and Adam got to know John's son Ben in College. They had gone a few times to Ben's home and had spent time getting to know the Senator. Jack appreciated that he was a straight up kind of guy just trying to do his best for the people.

"Yes they are. Ben just finished his MBA at Harvard, and has started his own consulting firm. I think you boys inspired him." The Senator winked at Jack as a large smile lit up his face.

"Ben has always been a smart guy. He'll do well."

"Yes he is. He said to tell you boys he wished he could have been here tonight. He wanted to stick close to home as his wife is expecting their first baby any day now."

"I can relate to that nervous first-time father feeling." Adam said looking across the room at his very pregnant wife. "I'll need to get in touch and offer him my congratulations."

"Do that. He'd love to hear from you."

"John you must have a busy schedule." Jack switched the topic of conversation. "I've been hearing good things from friends and family about recent speeches on your platform for stricter measures against human trafficking and other illegal activities." Jack rubbed his jaw remembering his own run-in with those thugs.

"I'm glad for the support." The Senator sighed. "But as you know those speeches come with backlash from the opposition."

"True. Has someone messed with you lately?"

"Well, there has been a problem of someone tampering with my papers." John looked back and forth between Jack and Adam. "I've noticed some of my documents have gone missing. The papers that have disappeared are important evidence against a political figure exposing his involvement in human trafficking. I really don't like the idea of someone trying that again."

"The police are looking into it?" Adam asked.

"Yes, they are so that's good. But I'm not comfortable just leaving it at that. I was wondering if I could ask you to stop by sometime Jack so we could discuss new designs for my house. Possibly adding one of those secret rooms that you design so well?" John ran a hand through his black-grey hair.

Jack could tell he was worried. "Of course. Why don't I stop by early next week and you can tell me what you're thinking?"

"Yes, that's perfect. Thanks. You're a lifesaver Jack." John let out a long sigh of relief. Adam spoke again. "There was someone else I wanted to introduce you to John if you don't mind?"

"No, not at all. See you next week, Jack." John shook his hand and walked away with Adam.

Jack took a glass of water from a waiter and looked around the room. His sister-in-law was talking to another one of her friends.

Elle motioned for him to come over. Jack walked toward her already wishing this evening was over. "Jack, I'd like you to meet a friend of mine. This is Julie Jones."

"Hi Julie, nice to meet you." Jack reached out and shook her hand.

"You as well, Jack. Thank you for the invitation. I've enjoyed connecting with the business leaders here tonight and of course Senator Carver. It's always good to meet new people, especially when you're in business like I am." A tight smile graced her lips.

Her features were business-like and controlled much like the perfect navy blue jacket and matching skirt she wore.

They talked for a few minutes. Jack soon discovered that she was hyper focused on how people saw her. Memories of how focused his first wife was on appearances came back to him. Jack determined that he'd get to know Julie as a friend, but would not pursue a relationship beyond that.

Soon, Elle's other friends joined the conversation. Nancy, was friendly but her chatter and tittering laughter put him on edge. Amy seemed like a nice teacher, Jack made a mental note to take the time to get to know her.

Admittedly, it'd been years since he'd talked to a woman for any reason other than business. It felt a little like learning to walk all over again.

Jack reminded himself, he wasn't interested in falling in love.

He decided he would get to know these women, make Elle happy and see if he could find a woman who would agree to a marriage of convenience.

Remembering how the scar on his face negatively affected women in his past, Jack did his best to make sure he was standing so people he talked with faced his left side. That was the side of his face without scars.

Before long, the caterers announced dinner. Jack

forced a smile, hiding the nervous ache that settled in his belly.

All this focus on finding a woman to marry was getting to him. He just needed to make it through the rest of the evening and he'd be fine.

Jack forced himself to talk to the woman on his right. Elle had arranged the seating at the dinner table, he was sure of it.

He saw Dunlin Campbell seated beside Maisie Merriweather both laughing like the siblings they were. Adam and Elle were talking with Senator Carver and his wife. Jack felt a little out of his element encircled by women he barely knew.

Jack reminded himself that this was only for tonight's dinner, then he could breathe easy again.

"Amy, how is it going teaching Paradise Lake's young minds?" Jack picked up his drink and took a sip as he looked at the lady beside him.

"Ah… " She stuttered and stared at him, her mouth dropped down in disbelief and horror. Jack forgot when he turned to face her, his scar was in plain view.

He wasn't surprised at her knee-jerk reaction. He'd seen similar responses dozens of times in the last four years.

Her cheeks turned red and she refocused her eyes on something just above his head as she replied. "It's going good. The children are great. I love teaching them."

"Good. I'm sure the children are all the better for having you for their teacher." Jack did his best to add to their polite conversation.

Finally, after a few minutes of strained replies and

lackluster conversation, Jack was grateful when the person seated next to Amy struck up a conversation with her.

As the caterers served coffee and desert, Jack turned to his left and found Bella talking with his friend Andrew Westcott. The muscles in his face tightened as he watched them talking together.

"So, that's why I started my online bookstore." Bella explained before she reached for her drink and took a sip. Andrew was interrupted by the woman on his left.

"I didn't know you had an online bookstore, Bella." Jack took that moment to insert himself into the conversation. For some reason, he felt irked that his friend was having a cozy conversation with Bella.

"Yes, I do Jack." Her big brown eyes lit up with an unreserved passion for her topic. "I've discovered people appreciate help when they can't find the rare print books they are searching for. My father's search for rare books on historic inventions and inventors got me started. Are you interested in rare books?"

Jack edged closer to Bella. Her unrelenting stare disconcerted him for a moment. She was looking at the right side of his face and had yet to recoil in disgust. Other than his GrandMom, Mom and Elle, Jack was sure Bella was the only other woman to see past the ugly scar.

Inhaling a quick breath, he forced his gaze away for a moment tamping down a longing for more of her sweet nature. He refocused on her question before he looked at her again. "I do like rare books. I have quite a collection in my own Library."

"Really? I'd be interested in seeing it some time." Bella

tilted her head to one side her gaze taking on a new sparkle.

"Since everyone is finished eating we could go there now." Jack stood up and the chatter around the dinner table lessened. "If anyone wants to see the Library, just follow me. Otherwise, feel free to make yourselves comfortable on the outside deck or in the great room."

Only a handful of people followed Jack and Bella into the Library.

Jack led them down the hallway of the sprawling log house he had built and opened the double doors to the large room.

A large log fireplace was at one end surrounded by a set of leather couches and chairs with a rustic coffee table between them.

Dominating one side of the Library, was a massive picture window with an incredible view of the lush green mountains. The beautiful view of nature seemed to go on forever.

Jack pointed out the different sections along the walls and the middle aisles where there were more bookshelves. "I've organized my Library into nonfiction and fiction, with a special section for rare print books over here." He walked toward a bookshelf that was wider and longer than any of the others.

"If any of you like James Bond movies, you'll appreciate this first edition of *Casino Royal* by Ian Fleming here." Jack held up a small grey book with a picture of a girl and a gun on it's cover. "This book was the first novel in the James Bond series published in April 1953."

"That's a great series." Andrew Westlock held the delicate book in both hands, his fingers skimming through the pages.

"And you might remember a little fantasy novel called, *The Hobbit* by J.R.R. Tolkien? This book cover - the one that has mountains in the background - is a first edition. Only fifteen hundred copies were printed when it was first published in 1937." Jack pointed to a book that looked like a hand-drawn picture of mountains and trees with black birds flying in white clouds above.

"Oh, I must've read this book five times when I was a kid." Amy Lewellyn skimmed through it's pages.

"These first editions are somewhat hard to find. I like the challenge though, so I continue to look for rare books." Jack continued to talk about other books he'd found and added to his collection.

"I've always dreamed of owning a first edition of *Pride and Prejudice* by Jane Austen. When I discovered her books as a teenager I devoured every one of her books until I'd read them all." Bella glanced up at him pink blossoming on her cheeks. She turned back to study the rare books, her eyes widening as she looked at the sheer number of books in his collection.

Jack looked up to see his Library suddenly empty of everyone except him and Bella. "Looks like everyone has left. I must have talked a long time."

A smile dangled on the corner of her lips. "No, I think we are the only ones really interested in these rare books. I find it all very fascinating. My Dad likes these old books too, especially the ones on science or inventions."

"Yes, that's how we connected years ago." Jack furrowed his brow as memories of that time surfaced.

Quickly he turned the conversation from the past to the present. "Your Dad still gives me ideas for the Science and Inventors online monthly magazine."

"Yes, my dad is full of interesting ideas." Her big blue eyes filled with trust and innocence looked up at him. She smiled and twirled a silky strand of her waist length brown hair. Jack wanted to bury his hands in her hair and feel the softness against his cheek.

Mentally Jack scolded himself. *Stop thinking about Bella like that. Her father is a friend who also works for you. What would Bella's Dad think if he knew you desired his daughter? Most likely he'd see it as a betrayal of your friendship.*

Jack breathed in Bella's flowery scent.

Forcing a slow gait, he followed behind her. He couldn't allow himself to think about a relationship with someone who could never be his.

"We appreciate that you invited both of us here tonight." Bella bit her lip and looked up at him.

"Glad you could come tonight." Jack stuffed his hands into his pockets to stop himself from pulling her into an embrace.

Her full red lips beckoned to him and he wanted to taste their sweetness. His awareness of her went into overdrive whenever she was near.

He stepped closer and impulsively reached out a hand to touch her hair. Thick strands of wavy brown hair fell like silk through his fingers.

Lifting up the ends of her hair to his nose, he breathed in the aroma of flowers. His favorite scent of roses pulled him in, reminding Jack of all the things he loved.

Bella peered up at him, her wide-eyed gaze filled with questions.

Unexpectedly, footsteps thundered down the hallway and the Library door opened. Jack dropped her hair like his hand was on fire.

"Bella, you need to come quick! It's your father." Andrew stood at the door, out of breath from running.

"What happened?" Bella rushed toward him her face white.

Jack hurried behind them down the hall.

When they got to the great room, Bella ran toward her father who lay back in Adam's arms. Bella sobbed as she knelt beside her Dad. "What happened? What's wrong with him?"

"We've already called the paramedics. The EMS team will be here soon. Your dad was complaining of pain in his chest. He had difficulty breathing so I gave him an aspirin." Adam spoke in soft tones to Bella and it seemed to calm her.

It was only a few minutes later that the medics rushed through the door. They checked his vitals and lifted Dunlin gently onto the flat canvas.

The medics covered Dunlin with a blanket and started rolling the stretcher out to the waiting ambulance.

Bella hurried after the medics only once looking back at Elle, Adam and Jack. "Thanks for your help. I'll be with my Dad."

Sharp pain twisted like a jagged knife in Jack's heart at the sight of her downcast eyes and pale cheeks.

"I'm going with Bella. I'm the only family she has."

Maisie slipped on her shoes and hurried out the door to catch up with her niece.

Everyone bustled frantically around Jack. Mrs. Potter was organizing the maids to clean up the dishes. Her grandson Chipper was busy carrying more finger food snacks and drinks to the side tables.

His personal assistant was doing his best to explain to the guests what happened, encouraging them to stay back.

By the time Jack turned his head to see Bella and Maisie, they had gone. He rushed out the door just in time to see the ambulance driving away.

Jack stood there on his front driveway staring after them, hands in his pockets.

For the first time in a long while, he felt unsure of what to do. His emotions were mixed. Up to now, he'd only wanted to hide away from the world. He told himself he didn't care about people other than his own family.

But, all he could remember in this moment were Bella's big brown eyes filled with tears. Bella looking pale as her hands wrung together. Bella standing motionless, her hands clenched together in a tight ball.

She'd looked so lost and alone.

Jack fidgeted, shifting his weight from one foot to the other.

He told himself he couldn't think about Bella right now.

Now was the time to focus and see how Dunlin was doing. He needed his creative works manager to be healthy and well enough to work, after all.

Jack needed him to finish the design project - the *Rose Adventure Park* - that project was on a tight deadline and it was critical they didn't miss it. Perhaps the reminder would spur Dunlin to heal faster.

He would go see him tomorrow.

Jack walked back into the house, happy with his decision.

There was only one problem: He couldn't get Bella's enchanting, heart-shaped face and large brown eyes out of his mind.

Every time he looked at her, her warm smile began to light up the dark places inside of him. Being around her compassionate nature, was poking holes in the brick walls he'd encased around his heart long ago.

Awareness of Bella filled him with fear and drew him to her all at the same time.

Jack wasn't comfortable with these new passions stirring inside of him. He forced them down, hoping they'd stay there.

There was no second chance for love... at least not for him.

ella

"YOUR FATHER HAD a non-ST elevation myocardial infarction. There was a partial block in one of his coronary arteries, which we have now removed."

The Cardiologist spoke in calm, soothing tones that Bella was sure came from years of telling people terrible news about their family members or loved ones.

She reached over and squeezed Aunt Maisie's hand as she listened, biting her lip wondering what horrible news the doctor would tell her next about her dad.

"But, he made it through surgery just fine."

At the surgeon's words, Bella wanted to give him a big hug. Instead, she sighed in relief and wore a sappy smile. It had been a little over seven hours of surgery and she had been on pins and needles the whole time.

Aunt Maisie had made several attempts to calm her by talking of other things. Her dear aunt had also done her best to distract her by offering to get tea more times than she could count.

Bella had managed to drink one cup of tea but refused the rest. She just couldn't hold anything down from worry over her father.

The doctor droned on. "That's the good news. But, you can expect it to take ten to twelve weeks for your dad to make a full recovery. He's been weakened considerably by this heart attack."

Bella swallowed to hold back tears that clogged her throat, at the doctor's words.

Her dad had always been the strongest man she knew. He was her hero. This was the man who had raised his only daughter since she was an infant.

Her dad was the guy who had taught her to play baseball and how to fish. He'd also taken her to the Library and to many bookstores growing up to challenge her mentally and to encourage her interest in stories and creative design.

The doctor's words describing her father as weak went against everything she knew about him. Bella shifted in her chair, brows puckered in worry as she mulled over the doctor's words.

"Most important to remember is that your father will need constant care and no stress whatsoever. He'll need to have his physical activity monitored. For now, he must only do light tasks or exercises. It's important to avoid doing anything that would bring stress to his heart."

The doctor paused, letting his instructions sink in. "There's also the chance that he could develop pneumonia. I would recommend having a family member or nurse care for him during the first six weeks that he's out of the hospital."

The cardiologist turned his tablet off and looked at them, his expression neutral.

"We'll do whatever needs to be done to help him get well." Bella's gaze shifted between the doctor and her aunt, her lips pressed tightly together.

She didn't know how they would make this work. She didn't know how they would survive now that her dad needed to be off work for months. Who knew how long it would take him to completely heal and recover?

And she didn't have a full-time job. She would need to find one quickly so they could pay their hospital expenses along with their bills from month to month.

Bella would do whatever she needed to, so that her dad was taken care of. After all, he had done so much for her. Now it was her turn to give back to him and to ensure her father had the care he needed.

"I'll arrange for the nurse to talk to you about care for your Dad."

"Thank you." Bella forced a confident smile on her face, even though her stomach knotted in fear.

The doctor nodded to both of them and strode from the room.

Aunt Maisie put an arm around her shoulders and pulled her close kissing the top of her head. "It'll be okay, you'll see. Your Dad is strong. Focus on the fact that he's alive. That's what's important."

Bella leaned her head on her aunt's shoulder, absorbing her strength.

Her aunt was a strong woman who fifteen years ago, had taken care of her husband in the last year before he died of cancer.

She knew what it meant to be strong and to sacrifice for people you loved. Her aunt might have exacting standards in many ways, but she was a staunch believer in family and that together they could make it through anything.

Bella sat back on her chair and squeezed her aunt's hand. She couldn't help but notice the tired lines around her aunt's green eyes and the wrinkled violet colored jacket with its untucked yellow blouse. The haphazard way her clothes hung on her, only highlighted the amount of stress she'd gone through.

"I know. I'm grateful Dad made it through surgery okay." She swallowed back emotion that clogged her throat. With one hand she rubbed a hand up and down her arm, trying to soothe her raw nerves. "I've been so afraid."

Bella took three slow deep breaths, doing her best to get her emotions under control. She looked at her watch and saw that it was six in the morning. They had been up all night and she was sure her aunt needed some rest.

"I'm going to wait here for the nurse and maybe get a little something to eat. But you should go home and rest Aunt Maisie." Bella was sure her aunt just needed a break.

"I'll do that sweetie. You'll call me when your Dad wakes up?"

"I promise."

"All right. It would be good to get a short rest and check on things. But I'll be back this afternoon to relieve you so you can sleep too." Her aunt stood up and Bella hugged her.

"Thanks Aunt Maisie. I don't know what I'd do without you." Bella kissed her cheek and was rewarded with a tired smile before her aunt walked down the hallway toward the exit. She stood there weariness pulling at her, but she couldn't give in. She needed to know more about her Dad.

Seeing the night nurse just finishing her shift, she walked up to her. "Do you think I could see my Dad?"

"Dunlin Campbell, right?" The red haired nurse clicked through the schedule on the computer. "Looks like Nurse Watkins is on duty. I'll buzz her."

It wasn't long before a matronly woman in a purple nurse scrubs approached Bella. "You must be Dunlin Campbell's daughter?"

At Bella's nod the nurse waved her to follow down the hallway. "Your dad will be happy to see you. He's been sleeping on and off since the surgery, but don't worry sweetie, that's normal."

Bella followed Nurse Watkins into a room at the far end of the hall.

Entering the room she saw that her Dad lay on the bed in a half-sitting position. Her hand reached up to cover her mouth at the sight of him. He looked so pale and helpless.

His normal neatly combed salt and pepper hair lay in a tangled mess. An oxygen tube was connected to her dad's nose and the bandages on his chest were intimidating and scary.

"Here you go, lovie." Nurse Watkins pulled up a chair beside the bed. "He'll wake up in a little while and you can talk to him then."

"Thank you." Bella forced her legs to walk to the chair. Sitting down, she kept her back ramrod straight. Her hands twisted together in a tight grip, her knuckles white.

Her movements were slow as she reached over and tucked her hand into her Dad's, giving his hand a gentle squeeze. "Hey Dad. Just wanted to let you know I'm here if you need me."

Uncertainty and fear crowded her thoughts as it suddenly hit her on a much deeper level, just how close her Dad had come to dying. For a moment she closed her eyes and heaved a couple of breaths, trying to bring her overwhelming emotions under control.

The nurse checked her Dad's pulse and the computer that monitored his heart. She typed a few things on the computer before turning to look at Bella. The nurse paused and smiled at her before she gently shut the door.

Watching the rise and fall of her Dad's chest was the one reassurance she was given in this day filled with uncertainty. The grey stubble on his chin, wrinkles on his face and dark shadows under his eyes reminded her that her dad was getting older. But, it also reminded her to make the most of every moment she had with him.

She held her Dad's hand and rested her head on her arm, soon falling asleep.

A large hand squeezed hers causing her to wake up.

Hearing the soft beeping of the monitor and seeing the stark white walls she felt disoriented for a moment.

Her father's raspy voice whispered her name. "Bella."

"Sorry Dad, I fell asleep. Let me get you some water." She reached over to the side table and poured water into a cup and held it for him until he finished drinking. His lips were cracked and dry and she reached into her purse and pulled out a soothing lip balm. Leaning over she rubbed it on his lips. "I hope that feels better."

He nodded. "I'm glad you're here. There's something I need to tell you."

"Dad you need to rest. That's more important right now."

"No, you don't understand." Her Dad furrowed his brow and looked up at the ceiling a faraway look in his eyes. "I'm under a very strict deadline to finish the design of the *Rose Adventure Park* for Jack. If I don't finish this design project in time, I'll lose all we have."

Bella pulled her chair closer so she could hear him better. "What do you mean? You work for Jack for a monthly salary, how could we possibly lose everything?"

Her dad gave her a sheepish look. "Not for this particular project. I chose to enter the closed competition that Jack was only offering to the top five designers in the nation. Maybe I was overly confident, but I really wanted to do this project. It has so many possibilities for creative expression and it's for kids. What could be more fun than that? When Jack asked if I wanted to enter a design for the competition, I jumped on it."

Bella's spine stiffened. She didn't like where this was going. "So you created a design, entered it and won."

"Yes. Jack gave the project to me. I signed the contract, began shaping the ideas and making them real. I also borrowed heavily to win the competition." Her dad sighed and waved a hand over the bandages that covered up the surgeon's large cut to his chest. "And now because of this, I won't be able to complete it on time. Which means I'm in big trouble."

"No you aren't Dad." Bella thought for a moment. "I'll talk to Jack. He knows you just had heart surgery, I'm sure he'll extend the deadline."

Her dad sighed. "If only it were that easy, Bella. No, if I don't finish this design project on time, Jack stands to lose millions and he'll also lose the project."

"How would he lose the project? I thought it was being built on his own land."

"Yes it is on his land, but for land within the town's jurisdiction, the town council has final say on land development. Jack explained to me that Paradise Lake town council is breathing down his neck about this project and some of the folks on the town council are opposed to the project."

"I guess that does put a different light on things." Bella puckered her brow in worry.

"Now that you've finished your degree in design, I want you to finish this project for me." Her Dad's grip on her hand tightened. "I don't trust this project to anyone else. You have to be the one to finish it."

"Dad, I don't know if I can…"

"Yes, you can. You've seen the designs for this project on my computer at work and at home. You've helped me figure out the new software too. I know you can do this."

The sparkle of unwavering belief in her Dad's eyes, which she'd glimpsed many times before, made her want to believe she could do this.

It was true that at the moment she was still only working part-time at the Library and she had no other job offers.

She was getting desperate for work. Problem was, she'd already refused Jack's job offer a few days ago. She wasn't excited about going back to Jack and eating humble pie. But she would do anything to help her Dad, even if it meant working for Jack.

Her Dad had poured himself into this project for the last two years and it was coming down to the final deadline. He had been so focused on these designs and yet she knew hardly anything about them. Bella realized she should have been more aware of her Dad's design projects.

Jack Stevenson was painstakingly specific about what he wanted and she'd heard that he'd fired many others who didn't meet his standards.

Sometimes Jack was too demanding of people around him. His pushy personality in combination with his scarred face had caused some people in their small town to call him the Beast.

She'd even overheard some of the moms of small children at the Library whispering that they didn't want their children near him.

It didn't bother Bella to see Jack's scar, she still thought him ruggedly handsome. But she found it irksome that he was so demanding.

Bella was intimidated by his exacting standards and

the very influential circles he was a part of. Jack had won numerous awards for his designs and she didn't know if she would be able to measure up.

So much about Jack Stevenson was far beyond her reach.

Jack would probably want someone else to take over this project.

Her belly tightened into a fist at the thought of taking on a massive design project of this size. It was a multi-million dollar project that involved people from many different fields all working together to complete this adventure park. This might be the only opportunity in her lifetime to work on a project this big.

If she did this well her resume had the potential to make her look attractive to the best design firms in the nation. That was really appealing.

But, the biggest reason she needed to do this was for her Dad. He was the most important person in her life. He'd sacrificed time with friends and had even given up jobs that paid more, so they could live near her aunt Maisie after her mother died. Her Dad must have known she needed a mother figure in her life, so they stayed. He'd done so much for her over the years that now it was her turn to take care of him.

Bella believed she could do this, but didn't know if Jack would hire her to take over for her Dad on this project. She threw her shoulders back determined to do everything she could to get Jack to hire her.

"I'll talk to Jack, maybe we can figure something out." Bella forced a smile as she looked at her dad. Inside she was a quivering mess at the thought of talking to Jack. But, she would ask Jack to have some grace with her father's contract, to hire her to take the project. How hard could that be?

A smile lit up her Dad's face. "Good. Now here's what you need to do. At my office, you'll find the designs that I've created so far under a file called Rose Adventure Park. You'll find the list of contacts there too. And there's more to tell you…"

"Ssh. Tell me later, Dad. Right now you just need to rest, so that your body can heal properly. I'll take care of everything." Bella leaned over and kissed her Dad on the cheek.

The corners of his lips turned up. "Thank you for doing this. You make me so proud."

With one hand she held his hand and with the other smoothed his brow until he nodded off. Looking at the needle in his arm, she was grateful for the pain medication that helped her Dad rest. She watched him for a few moments longer, thankful once more that her Dad was alive.

After his breathing deepened in a state of deep sleep, Bella quietly stepped out of the room.

As soon as Bella stepped outside the hospital, she dialled Aunt Maisie's number.

Waiting for her aunt to pick up the phone, she looked up only to see Jack standing there at the bottom of the stairs.

A tingling warmth skittered up her arms at the sight of him. Jack's brown hair was mussed up a little, but his beard was trimmed as usual. The corners of his mouth turned up slightly revealing pearl-white teeth and a pirate smile that made her weak in the knees.

"Hi. Dad's doing better and sleeping now so I thought I'd take a break. Aunt Maisie, could you pick me up and drive me home?"

It frustrated her that her dad's truck had been left at Jack's house, and she needed to rely on her aunt to get her home. She stopped a few steps before the bottom of the staircase, so she could finish talking to her aunt.

Bella was startled when suddenly Jack took the steps two at a time and reached his hand out for her phone.

"What are you…?" She hardly had the words out before he started talking to her aunt. Taking the phone out of her hand was one of those pushy and highhanded moves that she'd come to expect from Jack. Bella crossed her arms across her chest and tapped her foot on the stairs her irritation rising to new heights.

"Hi Maisie." Jack's arm rested casually on the stair railing as if he hadn't a care in the world. "Don't worry about it. I'll drive Bella home." Jack clicked the phone off and handed it back to her.

Bella tapped her foot. "What was that all about?"

"What?" His grin grew wider as he looked up at her. "I was just being helpful by offering to drive you home. Let's go."

Jack turned and walked down the staircase.

Bella followed unhappy and a little worried about being in close proximity to Jack. Opening the door to his blue truck, he offered his hand to help her up. She placed a tentative hand in his, a simple touch that sent waves of awareness through her.

"Thanks." She glanced up into hooded hazel eyes that studied her a little too closely.

As soon as she sat down Bella snatched her hand back, needing the distance between them.

When Jack was behind the wheel, he started the truck and turned to her. "How's your Dad really doing?"

Concern for her Dad was in the warmth of his tone. Bella peered over at him confused, feeling more at ease with the gruffer and disinterested Jack. "He's tired, but doing well."

At first he was highhanded, which she expected, then he suddenly swung the other way toward compassion. She was confused and didn't know what to make of him.

Jack drove out of the parking lot and toward her home.

Bella twiddled her fingers nervously on her lap, thinking maybe this was her chance to talk to Jack. "I talked with my Dad a little while ago when he first woke up. He mentioned the *Rose Adventure Park* project he's been working on."

Jack's shoulders stiffened and he expelled a breath. "Well, that project is a big concern now that your Dad's in the hospital."

"Maybe there's a solution."

Jack glanced her way his brow furrowed. "I'm listening."

Bella shifted her weight on the front seat. Looking out the window she rubbed clammy hands on her thighs. "Dad said he'd signed a contract for that project to meet the deadline which is only three weeks from now."

"Yes. And now I have no idea how we'll make the deadline."

Bella sighed and plunged ahead rubbing the moisture off her hands on her jeans once more. "Dad told me that when he signed that contract that he had specified that an assistant designer could take over and finish the project."

"Yes, only in a desperate situation."

"Well, with my Dad recovering from heart surgery, I think that qualifies as desperate."

Jack only grunted as he turned into the driveway that led up to her house.

"So, I wanted to ask you to have a little grace with my Dad's contract just until he's well enough to start work again. Meanwhile, I could work on the designs for the project."

"No." He parked his truck in front of her house.

"Why not? You said you didn't know how you'd make the deadline. Hiring a qualified designer will help you get it done."

"Yes, but you haven't worked on a project of this magnitude before." Jack's steady gaze seemed to pierce her own. "I'm not convinced you can do it."

Bella just stared at him suddenly feeling hot and cold all over. Her dad needed her to do this. "I realize I have a lot to learn, but I've been told from my instructors at college and other designers that I have great ideas and an eye for detail."

"I'm sure you do, but this is a huge project and something beyond your experience."

"I agree I have limited experience, but I'm convinced I can do this. My Dad signed that contract and I'm determined to do whatever I need to do to get this project completed by the deadline."

Jack's hazel eyes studied her for a full minute. The air was thick with tension.

Bella hated the fact that she was between a rock and a hard place. If she didn't get this job, her dad would not get paid and most likely go bankrupt.

Squaring her shoulders, she stared back at him.

After a long silence Jack spoke. "I'll agree to have you lead this project on two conditions."

"Okay. What are they?" Bella worried at what else Jack would require of her.

"First, I'll need you to live at my house so I can oversee every aspect of the project." Jack stared at her awaiting her response.

Bella hesitated. "I would agree, but I need to take care of my dad, so I don't see how I'll be able to do that. He's going to need my help when he's released from the hospital."

"If you agree to the second condition then your dad can live with us at my house and I'll hire a live-in nurse until he's fully recovered."

"Well then tell me what the second condition is."

"Marry me."

Shock rippled through her at his words.

Why would Jack make marriage to him a condition of getting the lead for this project? That she was confused and surprised was an understatement.

Though her heart shuddered in her ears like a loose wheel, she sat perfectly still and met his eyes with an unflinching stare. "Why are you making this a condition of my leading this project?"

Jack began by explaining his great-grandfather's will and the conditions of his inheritance. "As of today, I only have forty-five days left to marry and receive Grand's inheritance. If you agree, we would marry this week. We would agree that this is a marriage-in-name-only for one year."

"Your Dad would have the best care available and you would receive one million dollars to pay off any debt and give you security for the rest of your life. You would get half the money when we marry and the last half after we go our separate ways."

Bella looked away from him. Her belly clenched, knots of tension forming as she digested this information.

The idea of a marriage-in-name-only went against everything she dreamed of for herself.

She'd always wanted to marry for love. She'd always wanted to be independent. She'd always wanted to stop hiding in the shadows and be respected for who she was.

If she married Jack, her hopes for her future would be dashed.

"That's a very generous offer." Bella hesitated not wanting to say something that would ruin her chances of leading this project for her father. She was desperate for some time. "I really want my Dad taken care of, but I've always wanted to marry for love. I… need some time to think about your proposal."

She peered up at him, hoping he'd give her the time she needed to wrap her head around his unexpected proposal.

"You have until tomorrow morning." Jack got out of the truck and walked around to her door.

Bella had barely opened the door, when Jack held out his hand to help her down. Peering up at him she spoke, "I need more…"

Jack pulled her closer and leaned down, his eyes focused on her lips. Convinced Jack was about to kiss her, Bella turned her head to the side at the last minute. She wasn't ready for Jack's kisses.

His lips grazed her cheek and he whispered, "I'll pick you up at eight in the morning for breakfast. I'll be waiting for your answer."

Bella stood frozen to the spot as Jack tossed a half-smile her way.

As he got in his truck and drove away, she wondered how she was going to figure out her answer to Jack's marriage proposal in less than twenty-four hours.

CHAPTER FIVE

Jack

Jack drove up the driveway to Adam's ranch house and sat there a minute listening to the rain beating heavily on the windshield.

He was desperate to talk to his brother. He really needed to gain perspective on this whole situation with Bella.

Earlier when he'd texted Adam to ask if they could talk, he was relieved when his brother mentioned he had a free evening.

Jack opened the truck door and ran up the front steps in an effort to avoid getting wet.

Elle opened the door with a grin. "Come in, before you get soaked."

She waved him inside and closed the door.

"Hi Elle. You're looking good." Jack glanced at his sister-in-law's ever-growing belly.

"I appreciate you being nice about it, but I know I look like a beached whale. I'm really looking forward to when this baby is born." Elle rubbed her back with one hand. "I'm sure you're here to see your brother. Follow me. Adam's in his office fixing some bugs in his new software program."

She opened the door to her husband's office and Jack followed her inside. "Look who's here." Elle spoke and it wasn't until she touched his shoulder that Adam looked up. He got up, kissed his wife and stepped out from behind his desk to give his brother a quick hug.

"Jack, always good to see you."

"Thanks. You too." Jack paced the room, looking at the growing collection of horse racing trophy's that lined the front of the bookshelf. He picked up one of them, tracing it with his finger. "This is so great, Adam. Grand would say you're living in high cotton."

"Yeah. Elle's horse has been doing well. The trophy you are holding is last months win." Adam came and stood beside him with his hands in his pockets.

"It must be hard on Elle, not to be riding Justice for these races." Jack remembered how Adam's wife loved riding her horse.

"It is. But she knows that as soon as the baby's born and the doctor says it's okay for her to ride, she'll be able to ride as much as she likes." Adam patted him on the back and walked over to the large window that overlooked the barn and racetrack. "Riding Justice again will make Elle real happy."

"I'm sure it will." Jack stood next to his brother, his thoughts still on Bella.

"But you're not here to talk to me about that. I can tell something's troubling you." Adam stared at him for a long minute, knowing him well as only a close brother could.

"I need the advice and approval of my big brother." Jack leaned his shoulder against the wall, his hands in his pockets.

"Let's be honest, Jack. You've never been one to seek out the approval of others." Adam walked over to the countertop and started a fresh pot of coffee. "Even when we were kids you were more about jumping in head first or pushing the rest of us to do what you wanted."

Jack walked over to the leather couch and sat down, sighing. "Well, it looks like I might have done that again. Only this time I don't know if I pushed too far."

"Sounds serious. What happened?" Adam walked over and sat on the couch across from him.

"I told Bella that she was required to take over her dad's contract, or he would lose the project and any money he had coming to it. But, then I took it a step further."

Jack leaned on his elbows, toying with a pen. "I sort of convinced her it was in her best interest to marry me and live at the house. I offered to provide full time care for her dad, and one million dollars if she would agree to a marriage-in-name-only for one year."

"Hmm, that sounds somewhat familiar." Adam got up

and poured each of them a cup of coffee, setting them down on the coffee table.

"What can I say? I learned from the best."

"What did she say?"

"She thought about it for a minute and then asked for time to think about it. But she didn't look too happy."

"When I first suggested a marriage bargain, Elle wasn't too happy about it either." Adam took a sip of his coffee. "But at the time getting married was something that helped both of us."

Jack expelled a breath. "That's true for us too, but I don't know Adam. I might have pushed too far this time." Jack rubbed the back of his neck. "Bella might not trust me at all now."

"And that would bother you?"

"Of course it would. If we'll be working as a team on this design project and living day-to-day in the same house, we need to have at least a basic level of trust and friendship between us." Jack peered up at his brother who wore slight grin. "What?"

"If you care about Bella's feelings like you obviously do, then you'll do what's needed to talk things out so you can learn to trust each other."

"I'm not very good at that, I'm afraid." Jack gulped the rest of his coffee and stood up to take his cup to the sink. "I've been hiding in my cave ever since Elin and the baby died. I don't think I would even know where to begin."

Adam walked up to him and put his hands on both shoulders, looking him in the eye. "Start by choosing to listen more, demand less and put her needs before your own."

"Something you've been learning this past year?"

"Not always easy to do, but yes."

"I might not be too good at that." Jack looked out the window as he thought about how he could do that better with Bella.

"You don't need to be perfect. You just need to try."

Jack walked to the door before he turned to face his brother.

"You're a good man Jack. Now, you just need to help her see that." Adam's steady gaze held a knowing gleam that made him squirm a little inside.

Jack breathed a long sigh as his hand gripped the door-knob. Sending a shadowy smile Adam's way, he nodded and walked away deep in thought.

He would try to take his brother's advice, but he didn't know how. A gnawing that began in his belly worked its way up, the jagged edges slicing his throat.

Jack had a feeling that changing his ways would be just as impossible as a leopard changing its spots. But, he decided he was willing to try.

BELLA'S STOMACH was in knots as she watched Jack's truck disappear in the distance.

Turning, she walked inside the house and leaned her head up against the back of the door. Stunned by Jack's condition for her to take over her Dad's project, she stood motionless trying to take it all in.

Pacing back and forth in the kitchen, she searched to find the right answer. All she'd wanted to do was help her dad. Jack had finally agreed to let her take over the lead design on this project, but then he'd added those conditions.

The first one, living at Jack's house she was fine with as long as she knew her dad would be cared for. But the second condition — that she agree to a marriage-in-name-only — sent her reeling.

Pouring rain pelted the kitchen window, mirroring the pounding in her heart.

Desperate to talk to someone who would understand and help walk her through this, she thought of her best friend.

Elle. She had gone through her own struggles and marriage-of-convenience to Jack's brother Adam.

Finding her smartphone, she dialed her friend's number.

"Hey you. How are you feeling?"

"Bella, it's good to hear your voice. And to answer your question, I'm a little tired. But I hear that's normal when you're eight months pregnant." Elle laughed lightly. "Anyway, how's your dad doing?"

"He's on the mend. I'm so grateful he's still alive."

"I'm glad for you too. I hope you know that if you need anything, you can always let me know right?"

Bella grinned. "It's not like you don't have enough of your own concerns to deal with right now. But thanks Elle. I don't want to take up too much of your time, but do you have a few minutes to talk?"

"For you, of course."

"Something's come up and I really need some advice from someone who's been there."

"Uh oh. Sounds serious." Bella could hear shuffling noises in the background as Elle talked. "I'm just going to find a quiet corner to sit down and put my feet up. "Okay, let's hear it."

Bella twirled her hair and began telling Elle the conversation she'd had with Jack. "So, I don't know what to do. He offered to pay for a live-in nurse for my Dad if I agree to live in his house and take over the design project. I could do that, but it's Jack's second condition that's got me really worried. He wants a marriage of convenience, and I don't think I can do that."

"Hmm. That has a familiar ring to it." Bella heard a soft giggle on the other end of the phone line.

"Elle, this is serious. This is my life we're talking about here."

"I know. I'm sorry for laughing." The regret in Elle's tone, took away the sting of her laughter. "It's just too ironic that a marriage-in-name-only is your dilemma now much like it was mine a year ago."

"Agreed." Bella expelled a slow breath. "I'd do anything not to be forced into this contract with Jack right now."

"I get it, I really do. But if you think about it, if Jack wasn't in the picture right now, you'd still need to find some sort of work."

Bella knew that was true. As usual, her friend helped her put things in perspective.

Elle continued. "And it sounds like Jack's offer will definitely pay for all of your Dad's medical bills and you would have constant nursing care for him. At least that would be a burden off your shoulders."

Bella expelled a long breath. "Yeah, I know you're right."

There was a long pause until Elle spoke again, "Bella? Tell me why you're not speaking. What are you thinking?"

"It's just that I always wanted to marry for love. I can't help but feel sad and frustrated that I'm to marry to fulfill a contract. I feel so trapped." Bella curled up in her chair with one arm around her knees and the other holding her phone.

"It only feels that way right now. Remember it's only for a year then you'll have your freedom back, not to mention your father's medical bills and the mortgage will be paid."

Elle's words had a much needed calming effect. "That will be a relief." Bella stood up and came to a decision. "Okay you're right. It looks like the pros outweigh the cons by a long shot. I'll tell Jack I'll marry him."

"For what it's worth, I feel like you're making a good decision, Bella."

"I just feel very nervous and scared about the unknown part of my future."

"You'll be okay." Elle words brought comfort. "Deep down Jack's a good man. Try to be patient with him and do what you can to see past his gruff exterior. I have a feeling your kindness and compassionate heart is just what he needs to help heal the wounds in his heart."

"Maybe. I guess we'll have to see. Thank you Elle for helping me see this marriage contract in a better light." Bella could hear her friend's loud yawn over the phone line.

"I'm here to talk to you anytime, my friend."

"To bed with you, momma-to-be. I'll talk to you later." Bella waited until her friend hung up before disconnecting the call.

Out of habit she made tea, feeling very alone as she sat down at the table. She would need to check up on her dad tomorrow to see how he was doing.

Tomorrow. Her nerves did a somersault as she reminded herself tomorrow was the day she would say yes to Jack's proposal.

Her breaths grew quick and panicked and she took another sip of tea to calm her nerves. She thought of how abrupt Jack could be sometimes when he spoke.

Patience wasn't her strong suit, but she would need to take Elle's advice and try to be more understanding of Jack.

Bella had a feeling it would take a lot more effort than she realized.

SHE AWOKE the next morning to the bright sunlight slinking through her window. Turning to look at the clock on her nightstand she saw it was almost eight.

Panicking she jumped out of bed.

Jack was going to show up at her door soon.

She found her jeans and threw on her favorite yellow sweater.

Brushing her long dark hair, she swept it up in a ponytail leaving a few wisps spiralling down to her ears.

Bella had just reached the kitchen, when there was a loud knock on the door. Opening the door, her mouth fell open for a moment. Mason stood there waiting, hands in his pockets.

"Hi Bella."

After Bella had sufficiently recovered from the shock of seeing him there she responded, "Hi Mason. I'll step outside."

Bella slipped on her shoes, grabbed a sweater-jacket and stepped out onto the porch. There was no way she was going to invite Mason inside her Dad's house. She would hear what he had to say in the wide outdoors in full view of anyone who would happen to drive past their house.

"So, why did you stop by?"

"Bella is that any way to greet your old friend?" Mason leaned close whispering in her ear.

In her hurry to escape being anywhere near him, she almost tripped. "I'm just surprised to see you here."

"It's all right. I stopped by because I heard about your Dad. How's he doing?"

"I was able to talk to him this morning. He's doing as well as can be expected." Bella crossed her arms over her chest wondering at his unexpected concern.

"That's good to hear. But, I'm sure it doesn't help to have these unexpected medical concerns or bills." Mason stepped a little closer, his head cocked slightly to the side.

"No, but we'll figure it out."

"Well, I'd like to help. I'm able to now that I've been elected into this new job."

"New job?" Bella hadn't heard of anything new but she was sure she was about to get an earful.

"Didn't you hear? Just last week I was elected to serve

on the Paradise Lake town council. The Wolffe brothers used their considerable influence to sway votes in my favor." Mason's smug tone of voice and the way his body swaggered grated on her nerves.

"I didn't know that. Congratulations."

"Don't you see, Bella? Now that I have this new job with great pay and benefits we can get married. I remember you used to talk about getting married someday. Now we can."

Shocked into silence, Bella just stared at him. She couldn't believe he was still focused on the two of them getting married.

"Mason, that was High School. We were kids." Bella sighed still not quite believing they were having this conversation again.

"I've changed since then and so have you. I don't want to marry you Mason. I'm sure there's some other girl just waiting for you to sweep her off her feet."

Mason stepped closer and gripped her shoulders. She tried to step back but he held her firm. "Bella, I'm not giving up. One way or another I always get what I want. And this time I want you."

At the sound of gravel crunching under truck tires, Bella turned to see Jack's truck come up the driveway.

For once, the nearness of Jack made her sigh in relief. She turned back to Mason and decided it was time to be firm.

"Mason, I'm afraid you're too late. I've agreed to marry Jack Stevenson." It was true although she hadn't told Jack about her decision yet. Mason's lips drew together in a thin line and a tick formed in his clenched jaw.

His fingers grasped her shoulders even tighter. "You'll be sorry you chose him over me Bella."

"You're hurting me, Mason. Let go of me." Bella tried to pull away but Mason held her firm. Strong fingers dug into her skin and she winced in pain.

Suddenly strong arms reached out and grabbed Mason, pulling him swiftly off of Bella. "She won't be sorry. It's you who will be sorry if I ever see you manhandling my wife-to-be again. Do you understand?" Jack's deep voice thundered, tight lines forming around his mouth.

A sigh of relief flooded Bella as Jack stepped up to protect her. He'd called her his wife-to-be. Instead of feeling anger, an odd shiver of anticipation rose up inside her causing her skin to prickle with awareness. She stiffened at her body's betrayal. How could she feel that way when the last thing she wanted to do was marry him?

Mason shook himself free from Jack's grip and backed away. "I can see why they call you the Beast. You're just ugly all around. You might be marrying Bella, but it won't last. Who could stand to be married to a monster like you?"

Spinning his truck tires, Mason drove away spitting gravel as he went.

Bella was horrified at Mason's parting shot. She looked at Jack, his face was stoic and unreadable. From his unmovable features it seemed like this wasn't the first time he'd heard similar comments.

Jack turned his gaze searching hers. "Are you okay?"

"Yeah, I'm okay. Mason has been somewhat bothersome lately." Bella let out a nervous laugh looking away from him for a moment.

Jack studied her a moment longer. "Well, let me know if he bothers you again all right?"

His concern warmed her all over. It annoyed Bella that somehow this man had the ability to affect her. She needed to divert his attention away from her and onto something else.

She pulled at the long sleeves of her sweater, her gaze moving up to his. "I'll let you know Jack. But meanwhile, I'm hungry and you promised breakfast. Should we get going?"

"Of course." Jack put his hand on the small of her back as they walked to his truck. Warm tingles raced up her back at his touch.

Opening the truck door, he held her hand to help her inside.

He hurried to the driver's side, and drove off her yard and onto the highway and up the mountain road that led to his house. "Mrs. Potter, my housekeeper and cook, will be happy you're hungry. She's made a big breakfast."

Bella's nerves were ragged by the time they stepped into Jack's mansion on top of the hill. The size of his house was immense. It could easily pass for a hotel at least that was Bella's impression.

The last time she'd been here had been for the dinner, but everything from that night seemed to be a blur in her memory because of her father's heart attack.

Today, as she walked into the house she was able to appreciate the beautiful log walls, the massive windows and skylights that made the room so sunny and cheery.

They were met at the door by Jack's large Saint Bernard dog. The huge furry friend ran up to Bella, nearly bumping her over. "Brahms, where are your manners? Not so rough with the lady."

At Jack's firm voice, his dog groaned loudly bending low and stretching his paws out on the floor.

"Brahms, you are so big and adorable. Give me a hug." Bella whispered as she bent down, rubbing behind his ears. Jack's dog sat on his haunches and licked Bella's cheek as she wrapped both arms around him.

"Well, you've certainly made a conquest of Brahms. He's never been so friendly to someone he's never met before."

Bella stood to her feet, and sent Jack a sheepish smile. "What can I say? I really love dogs and Brahms is amazing."

"Traitor." Jack bent down and whispered to his dog before he stood up and turned toward Bella a half grin lifting the corners of his mouth.

Bella giggled. She found it funny that Jack felt his dog had betrayed him by liking her a little too much.

"Shall we?" Jack offered his arm and she slipped her hand in the crook of his arm as they walked toward the back of the house.

Soon they came to a small but sunny breakfast nook beside large windows that delivered an incredible view. Jack's housekeeper carried large covered plates and bowls and set them on the large wooden breakfast table.

"Mrs. Potter, I'd like you to meet Bella Campbell." Jack spoke to a short, gently rounded woman with grey hair and blue eyes.

"Miss Campbell, I hope you like the breakfast." Mrs. Potter's smile lifted her rosy cheeks.

Bella nodded. "Mrs. Potter, I'm sure I will. Thank you for putting together such a beautiful meal." Jack pulled out a chair for Bella to sit down.

Her stomach was doing flip-flops as nervousness got the better of her.

Staring out the large picture window, she hoped to chase away her jitters. Wiping her clammy hands on her jeans, she tried to forget about how uncomfortable she felt being here in Jack's home. But, since her conversation with Elle last night and her decision it seemed she would need to get used to it.

Inhaling a quick breath, she stared in amazement at the beauty of the view. In the far distance she saw the whole valley of Paradise Lake and the huge lake beyond. Green hills and valleys with an abundance of trees lay between Jack's mountain and the small town below.

Closer to Jack's house was a large backyard that boasted of a swimming pool and a tennis court, which was surrounded by beautiful multi-colored roses and other perennial flowers and shrubs.

"You like?" Jack's deep voice interrupted her reverie.

Bella turned to see Jack's steady gaze on hers. "It's really beautiful Jack. You seem to have created a wonderland of beauty right here in your own backyard."

"To be fair, I have a gardener that comes three times a week. He does most of the work that the rest of us just get to enjoy. That being said, I do love to surround myself with beauty." Jack's gaze focused intently on her. "Which brings me back to you."

Heat formed in her neck and shot up to her cheeks at his look of appreciation. She toyed with her fork and spoon while she waited for him to continue speaking.

"I'm eager to hear what you've decided about our conversation yesterday." Jack's steady gaze caused her to shift uncomfortably in her chair.

Jack was talking about marrying him.

He was offering her a way to pay off all their debts. It would be like a fresh start by the time the year was over.

Not only that, but after this morning's fiasco with her ex-boyfriend, she was convinced she'd be better off if she was somewhere where Mason wouldn't be able to try to get her to marry him.

For the peace of mind it would bring her Dad, she could do this. She would marry Jack. She would sacrifice her dreams for her Dad. It was the least she could do for the wonderful man who raised her and who had sacrificed so much for her.

Looking back at Jack, she nodded. "I can't believe I'm saying this, but yes I will marry you. But I have a condition of my own."

"What is it?" Jack's brow furrowed and the lines became more pronounced on his forehead.

"Since this is a fake marriage, I'm asking that somehow we let my dad and your family believe we got married because we fell in love." Her cheeks turned pink as she voiced her thoughts out loud.

Bella bit her lip and nervously picked imaginary lint off her sweater before she looked up at him.

"Agreed." Jack caressed her hand. "And I hope you don't mind if we don't invite that boorish lout who was manhandling you earlier today." Jack shook his head from side to side a heavy sigh escaping his lips.

"I agree. I really don't want to be anywhere near Mason again." Bella sent him a half-smile.

"Good. Now that we have that settled there's only one thing left to do." Jack stood to his feet and walked the few steps to where she sat at the end of the table.

Bending on one knee he reached for her hand and looked up at her a gleam in his eyes. "Bella Campbell will you marry me?"

Bella was frozen for a moment as she saw Jack Stevenson bending on one knee in front of her.

For a moment her imagination rushed ahead as if pretending this was a romantic proposal from a man who loved her, before she gave herself the harsh reminder that this wasn't real. This was only a fake marriage.

She slowly expelled a breath. "Yes."

Jack reached into his pocket and pulled out a beautiful diamond ring. It was a large marquis style with many tiny diamonds surrounding it.

He gently slipped it onto her ring finger. Holding her hand for a moment, his gaze raked her face studying her for a full minute before he stood to his feet.

For a moment, she could've sworn she saw fear in his eyes.

Bella shook her head, realizing her imagination was getting her in trouble again. Forcing herself to refocus, she took the napkin and cleaned the crumbs from around her plate.

Her future husband sat down at the end of the table.

Bella noticed how his eyebrows puckered and his eyes were dark and brooding as he stared into his coffee cup.

Looking once more at the shiny engagement ring, she turned towards her husband-to-be. "I've never had anything so beautiful Jack. Thank you."

"Well, now you do." Jack's sudden abrupt tone sent Bella's thoughts whirling. Questions rose in her mind. Why couldn't he accept a simple compliment? It dawned on Bella, that maybe by marrying her Jack was reliving painful memories of his first wife.

"Sorry Jack for being so thoughtless. I forgot about the fact that this day must remind you of marrying your first wife." Bella's voice shook a little as she peered over at Jack to see him gulp down the rest of his coffee.

He shifted uncomfortably. "Don't worry about it. But, if it's all the same to you, I'd rather not talk about that right now."

Without warning he stood to his feet and ran a hand through his hair. "Shall we talk about the other part of our contract?"

Bella stood up, her legs wobbly with the sudden change in Jack. He had began to open up to her and just as suddenly put walls between them. "Sure."

He turned, waiting for her. "Follow me and I'll show you to your new office."

Bella stayed close to Jack's side as they walked awestruck by the sheer size of the house. It would be really easy to get lost in a house this size.

As they walked down the hallway in the west wing, he pointed out the Library and the Conservatory, which she had already seen last time.

"My office is next to the Conservatory. At the end of the hall your bedroom is across from my own." Heat rose up in her cheeks at his announcement. "Your father's room and his nurse's room are next to yours. But the room next to mine is locked. I've told everyone in the house, no one is to go in there. Other than that you are free to explore the house."

Bella couldn't help being curious about the room that was locked. What did Jack keep hidden in there? She reminded herself that it was none of her business. This was to be a fake marriage anyway.

She followed Jack farther down the hallway until he opened the door to a room across from his office. The space was big with two large windows, a desk and a lot of shelf space.

"What do you think?"

"It's sunny and bright in here Jack. I love it." Bella walked to the window that looked across a wide expanse of green lawn and trees. It was a peaceful scene. "When did you want me to get started?"

"First we'll marry. Since your Dad is home from the hospital at the end of next week, why don't we get married here next Saturday?" Jack announced their wedding in a detached tone of voice.

"Next Saturday is much too soon..." Bella sputtered about to argue when Jack interrupted.

"Remember, we're on a tight deadline here." He looked at the calendar on his smartphone. "We need to get the wedding over with, so we can have a short research trip and return home to get the Rose Adventure Park design finished and approved by the town council. We don't have any time to lose."

"You're right of course. We'll let our family and close friends know the wedding will be on Saturday." Bella pressed her lips together. Her shoulders stiffened at Jack's reminder that they were just getting the wedding over and done.

She was fit to be tied as Aunt Maisie would say.

Her throat was parched and raw as she followed Jack out of the office. She wondered, not for the first time, how she would be able to handle being close to her prickly husband-to-be for any length of time.

But, it was too late. She had committed to marry him.

Making sacrifices didn't frighten her. Not being there for her Dad when he needed her, did.

She would sacrifice herself for her Dad and marry Jack. What could possibly go wrong with a marriage contract to the beast?

CHAPTER SIX

Jack

Jack's gaze widened and his belly tightened in knots as he watched the beautiful woman in the long white wedding gown glide down the staircase.

Bella had only just agreed to marry him a week ago and today she was becoming his wife.

Only two days ago, her dad moved into Jack's house. Everything in his life had changed so quickly.

Bella walked down the staircase in her mother's lacy wedding gown looking more beautiful than any woman he'd ever seen.

Jack swallowed a lump of emotion that had somehow clogged his throat. Bella was too beautiful to be marrying him -- a man who folks around town called the beast.

But he needed to do this. It was only for a year. After that both of them would be free of this marriage-in-name-only. Jack convinced himself that he'd be happy to be free of the marriage shackles when the time came.

Yet, if he really believed that, why did his heartbeat accelerate like a runaway race car?

Jack stood motionless, his eyes riveted on his future wife. Bella reached the bottom of the staircase and rested her hand on her Dad's arm. Her Dad looked up from his sitting position in his wheelchair smiling up at her. She wore a tender smile on her beautiful face as she bent down and kissed his cheek.

Dunlin Campbell's nurse Marmie, guided his wheelchair to the front of the room as Bella walked alongside with her hand on her Dad's shoulder.

Jack stared at his bride, mesmerized by every part of her features. Her graceful walk, her womanly figure and her thick brown hair that fell in silky waves to her waist. His knees weakened and he stood frozen staring into her upturned face with those expressive dark brown doe eyes.

Finally his bride stood in front of him. Large eyes filled with uncertainty stared back at him.

His bride-to-be's father moved closer to Jack.

"Take good care of my daughter Jack." Dunlin Campbell sat in his wheelchair, his wide green eyes studying him. Jack saw real concern there. He knew what Bella's Dad was really asking. If something went south with his health and he was no longer around for his daughter, would Jack make sure she didn't have to worry? The answer of course, was yes.

He reached down and gripped Dunlin's hand in a firm

handshake. "I promise."

Dunlin's wide smile revealed his pleasure. He placed his daughter's hand on top of his own.

Bella reached down to kiss her Dad's cheek once more before she looked back up at Jack.

Her body teetered slightly and she placed a hand on her Dad's wheelchair for support. Jack tucked one hand around her slender waist and pulled her to his side.

Her cheeks blossomed in a flurry of pink.

As they spoke their vows, Bella's cheeks remained a delightful rose color.

All too soon the wedding ceremony came to a close.

"You may kiss the bride." The pastor's words brought a jolt of awareness to Jack.

Bella's gaze remained glued to his, unreadable. He wondered what was going through her mind. When Jack had first talked about marrying, Bella had stated emphatically that she wanted her Dad and his family to believe they were marrying for love.

Even though Jack was convinced he would never fall in love again, he was ready to make their families believe they had fallen in love. He'd agreed to do it for Bella.

Jack leaned down slowly taking in every curve of her face. With one hand on her waist he pulled her close and with the other hand he tilted up her chin.

His heart pounded hard and slow as he leaned closer, focused on the fullness of her lips, until his mouth touched their sweetness.

Bella's lips melted deeper into his own until he didn't know where hers began and his ended.

Heat curled in his belly, turning into hot molten liquid.

All thoughts of anything else faded away replaced by the increased pounding of his heart in his ears. Desire seeped into his belly like an injection of hot lava.

The sweetness of her warm lips made him feel like he was falling.

Bewildered at his response to his new wife, he forced himself to step back. He stared down at Bella, shocked and confused all at the same time.

Sudden thoughts swirled in his head — a pathetic, panicky kind of denial of what just happened — and a tingling sensation crept up his spine touching the back of his neck.

Jack's growing awareness of his new bride was beginning to cause more trouble than he'd originally planned. Mixed emotions ran through him like a train wreck barrelling down an unfinished track, without a clue about how he was going to stop the collision.

An overwhelming sense of panic flooded him.

He forced a smile on his lips, but his insides were churning and unsteady.

❧

BELLA'S KNEES turned weak from Jack's passionate kiss, but just as quickly her new husband stepped away.

Her trembling fingers touched her lips and a tingling warmth cascaded through them.

For a moment she didn't move, couldn't breathe as she peered up at the stoic countenance of her new husband. The only sign that he felt anything was a slight tick in his set jawline.

Jack's hooded gaze peered down at her for a moment longer before offering her his arm.

The room that had been quiet until now, suddenly burst forth into a hubbub of sound. The background music grew louder. The wedding guests clapped.

The pastor pronounced them husband and wife. "Ladies and gentlemen, introducing Jack and Bella Stevenson."

A rush of heat spread up her neck to her cheeks as she saw Jack's family, her dad and their friends glancing between her and Jack.

Jack stepped closer to her side, his hand tucking hers more firmly into the curve of his arm as they walked down the aisle toward the back of the room.

Bella pasted on a smile and peered up at Jack.

Her new husband gave her a barely-there-smile. The look in his eyes resembled a sort of deer-in-the-headlights look of surprise.

She was relieved when family and other wedding guests interrupted them. "Oh Bella, I'm so happy. Now, we're truly sisters." Her best friend Elle wrapped her arms around her and kissed her cheek and whispered. "Jack keeps looking at you like a man who doesn't know what just hit him. I think he's falling for you."

Elle stepped back and rubbed her baby bump a playful smile hovering on her lips.

Rolling her eyes, Bella let her friend know she didn't believe a word of it.

Jack had only proposed because he wanted his inheritance and she had agreed because that was the only way she could finish her Dad's contract. They'd agreed to a fake marriage and as far as she could tell, Jack didn't harbor any romantic feelings for her.

Bella gave Elle a weak smile reminded of the uncertain future that loomed large on the horizon. "We'll talk later. You know I adore you for being such a good friend."

"Love you too, sis." Elle leaned over and kissed her cheek before she moved on.

Soon, Bella was hugged and kissed by Jack's brothers Adam, Gabe, Luke and Zach.

Gabe gave her a big hug, his words a half whisper, "Don't let Jack run you over. Let him know how you feel. He needs someone in his life to help keep him in check."

Heat flushed Bella's cheeks. "I'll do my best."

"Gabe what sort of lies are you mumbling into my wife's ear?" Jack place a large hand around Bella's waist pulling her close to his side and kissing the top of her head.

Warm tingles skittered from her waist where Jack's hand rested all the way up to her neck. Even as insecurities plagued her about marrying Jack, her body betrayed her at the pleasure of his touch.

"Aww, my dear. It's so wonderful to have another daughter in the family." Eliza Stevenson embraced her with a gentle hug. "I'm not surprised Jack snatched you up and married you quickly. You're beautiful Bella and he's in love. Once my son knows what he wants, he chases after it with intense focus."

"Thanks for your kind words, Mrs. Stevenson." Bella pulled back, a wobbly smile plastered to her lips. A deep longing stirred inside her at her mother-in-law's words. She realized how much she wished her words were true.

But the sad reality was, Eliza's words weren't true.

She rubbed clammy hands along the sides of her wedding dress unsure of what to say.

"Please Bella, call me Mom or Eliza." She leaned over and kissed her cheek. "I'm really looking forward to getting to know you better."

Jack's grandmother came to stand beside Eliza with Jack's grandfather right beside her. "I second that. It's wonderful to celebrate this day with you and Jack." Catherine Stevenson put her hands on her shoulders and kissed her cheek.

"Thank you, Mrs. Stevenson."

"Now that you're part of this family, call me Grandmom my dear." She turned her head to look at her husband. "And call my husband Granddad just like Jack does. You're part of our family now."

Tears smarted in her eyes at how easily they welcomed her into the family.

"I will." Bella was suddenly overcome by guilt at the welcome she received from Jack's mom and Grandparents. They saw her as a woman that Jack married for love, when in her mind nothing could be further from the truth.

Jack saw marrying her as a way to get his hands on his inheritance. But she couldn't fault him for it because they both benefited from this fake marriage.

It was Jack's offer to let her take over her dad's contract, that would allow her to pay off their debt and pay for a nurse for her dad that made her think this marriage contract was a good idea.

Still, with their parents and grandparents convinced

this marriage was a love match, it was more important than ever for her and Jack to make them believe they loved each other.

Memories of his kiss made her want to believe in a forever kind of love.

When Jack pulled her close to his side and leaned over and kissed her cheek, she had to remind herself that this relationship wasn't real. Her new husband was just acting the part of a man in love.

"Ah, young love. Those were the good ol' days, right sweetheart?" Jack's Granddad smiled mischievously at his wife and turned to wink at Bella.

"Those days were good, but now we have a love that is stronger. And you two will have a strong love too, as you continue to show your love daily to each other." Catherine pulled Jack into an embrace and kissed his cheek.

"That's the fun part." William winked at Bella and Jack.

Bella caught the flush of pink that rose up on Jack's GrandMom's cheeks and grinned. Seeing their loving banter with one another was something Bella realized she had missed in her childhood.

Her mother died when she was born and all but one of her grandparents had passed away. She never had the chance to see an example of love and commitment from parents or grandparents as a child.

An unfamiliar longing rose up inside her. It was the kind of ache that could only be satisfied by being part of a family that loved her.

She watched her Dad as his nurse pushed his wheel-chair beside her. With her Dad and Aunt Maisie showering so much love on her, she had a lot to be thankful for.

Leaning over, Bella gave her Dad a big hug. "Dad, I just want to let you know how much I love you and how grateful I am for you."

"Ah Beauty. I love you too." A sheen of tears moistened Dunlin Campbell's eyes. He was a big strong man who didn't share his emotions freely. When he did, there was a depth of meaning behind it. "You're so beautiful standing here in your mother's wedding dress. Seeing you wearing it, brought to mind so many wonderful memories of when I married Isabella Rose. Not only do you have your mother's name but also her beautiful face and form. She would have loved to see you wearing her dress and marrying Jack today."

"Oh Dad. I wish she could've been here today too. But, I'm thankful we carry the wonderful memories of mom in our hearts." With a gentle hand her father wiped a tear that ran down her cheek.

"You've the right of it, lassie. I think she's looking down from Heaven today, a big smile on her face."

"I think so too. You're beautiful Bella." Aunt Maisie came up behind her Dad and wrapped Bella in her arms.

"Thank you Aunt." Bella sighed in her aunt's arms. "I'm glad you're here."

"Well where else would I be, when my only niece is getting married?" Aunt Maisie ran her hands gently down the lace sleeves of her mother's wedding dress a wistful smile on her face. Her brow puckered in concern as she looked deep into Bella's eyes and leaned close to whisper. "I just want you to know you can talk to me about anything okay?"

"I know and I appreciate that. Thanks, Aunt Maisie."

Bella forced a smile. She understood the hidden meaning behind her aunt's words. Her aunt wondered why she married Jack without so much as giving her a hint that anything was going on between them.

An uncomfortable wave of warmth brushed her neck and face. It seemed she was stuck between a rock and a hard place. Her aunt wanted to know the whole truth, but she couldn't tell her because of loyalty to Jack.

Relief washed over Bella as her aunt turned to talk to Jack.

Soon more friends came to wish them well.

Rory gave her a big hug. "This wedding was quite a surprise, but I couldn't be happier for you." Her friend stepped closer and whispered. "Just to give you a heads up, there's one mutual friend that is very unhappy to hear of your wedding."

Mason. Bella cringed a little on the inside. Her old high school boyfriend was a nuisance that continued to plague her.

"But he already knows I'm not interested in him. I spoke to him only a week ago."

"I know, but I'd still be on the lookout for him. Remember what you told me happened in High School?" Rory pointed out an incident that Bella wished she could erase from her memory.

They had been in their senior year and Bella had just broke up with Mason. She wasn't sure what happened, only that her ex-boyfriend seemed to come unhinged from their breakup. He became really mean to her and told embarrassing stories about Bella's father that weren't true.

Soon she heard rumors spreading from every direction that her Dad was a mad scientist. It wasn't long before her friends started asking if everything was okay with her Dad. She didn't want to have to deal with him again.

"I remember." Bella sighed.

"I just hope he doesn't create new problems for you."

"Well, I'm not going to worry about Mason. I've got enough things going on in my life to handle right now, without adding more." Bella sighed clenching her hands together. "But thanks for letting me know."

"Of course. And in case I didn't tell you, you look great today. I'm so happy for you." Rory kissed her cheek and moved away to talk to other people. Bella breathed a sigh of relief when she'd finished talking with most of the guests that came to their wedding.

Knots of anxiety formed in her stomach from everything that was going on in her life.

Finishing her father's contract with Jack was Bella's biggest concern right now. Her new husband was a handsome man despite his scar, but his gruff and overbearing personality overwhelmed her. She would need to learn how to stand up to Jack.

Her hands trembled at her side and she gripped the lacy material of her mother's wedding gown.

How was she supposed to do this for an entire year?

JACK SIGHED in relief as soon as he finished talking with the small group of family and friends that had shown up to their wedding.

Bella had wanted a simple and private ceremony and having the wedding at his home in the mountains seemed ideal for that.

He was now married to Bella Campbell - er, Bella Stevenson.

Jack glanced over at the beautiful woman who was now his wife.

Brown hair hung in waves over her shoulders and down her back. Beautiful silky waves. He lifted his hand and twirled a handful through his fingers. Bella turned and peered up at him, doubt and uncertainty in her gaze. Her hands continued to fidget with her wedding dress.

It suddenly struck Jack that perhaps this day had been a bit much for her. "Come with me. I want to show you a perfect place to relax."

Jack grasped Bella's cold hand and they walked down the hallway and through French doors. The room was a Conservatory that opened up to a large balcony.

The sweet smell of roses filled the room.

He tugged on Bella's hand and walked with her until they stood in the middle of the greenery. Jack knew bringing his new wife here was the right choice when eyes widened and a slow smile formed on her lips.

Bella stood motionless for a moment inhaling the scent of the tall green vines and perennial plants that surrounded every corner of the room.

"This is so beautiful Jack. Such wonderful smells in this room. I smell lemon, chocolate, rose and herbal type scents." Bella stepped closer to the plants that were woven through the wooden lattice.

"This is a scented geranium and this plant has that chocolate fragrance." Jack pointed to a leaf shaped like lace. "Next to it are citrus blossoms, which is that lemon scent you smelled earlier. And over here, this shrub like tree is a sweet bay, which gives off a savory herbal scent."

Bella walked up to each of the plants running her fingers along their velvet tips, her eyes closed breathing in their aroma, a small smile on her lips.

Jack watched her with his hands in his pockets. "Just take a moment to breathe in the beauty of the flowers and relax from the stress of the day."

"How did you know this is what I needed?" Bella turned and looked up at him, her gaze thoughtful and full of questions.

"You get a line between your eyebrows when you're worried about something. You had it when you stepped out of the hospital from seeing your dad and you have that same line now." He reached over and traced a finger gently down the lines in her forehead trying to erase the grooves.

Bella shivered at his gentle touch. She closed her eyes and sighed. "I feel better already."

"Good." Jack stood there a moment looking at her beautiful face, loving the feel of her soft skin unmarred by flaws or scars. He wanted to lean down and kiss the end of her nose, her pink cheeks and rosy red lips, but stopped himself as soon as that thought entered his mind.

He jerked his hand away not liking the direction of his wayward thoughts.

Jack walked over to the middle of the room where there were many different varieties of rose bushes. He picked up a deep pink colored rose and with the small plant scissors he kept in the Conservatory, snipped off a rose with the fullest blossoms.

"This is one of the most exquisite rose bushes in the Conservatory. My mother who loves to grow roses started this deep pink-purple strain." Jack breathed deeply of its scent a slight smile on his face. He handed the rose to her, his gaze focused on her delicate features.

"For you. Its beauty doesn't do you justice."

A surprised wonder lit up Bella's face and a single tear slipped down her cheek.

His wife held the rose between her fingers and touched her nose to the tip of the rose, breathing in the sweet aroma. "This is heaven on earth. Thank you Jack. You just made this day perfect."

Jack sucked in a breath, uncomfortable with the mixture of emotions that washed over him. Suddenly he was aware that he was happy to have pleased his new wife.

It wasn't like him to want to please anyone. His own emotions and actions confused him. He had the reputation of a gruff and demanding man who lived as a hermit in the mountains. The fact was, he was used to people walking the other way when they saw him coming or just avoiding him altogether.

But, Bella's smile and her look of pure joy and happiness caused him to come undone. He didn't know what was happening to him. Jack only knew he wanted more of it, yet he was much too afraid of the power of these raw emotions to get too close.

How would he be able to guard his heart from his wife, when she was by his side everyday?

CHAPTER SEVEN

ella

"We'll be landing in Paris in fifteen minutes. Please fasten your seat belts." Jack's pilot announced their arrival and Bella's grip tightened on the armrests.

Ever since she was a little girl, she'd been afraid flying. Her stomach clenched as she looked out the window and saw how high in the air they were.

The private jet's engine droned on loudly as they descended. She still couldn't believe they were in France. Her body hummed with excitement.

Everyone had gone home late last night after the catered wedding meal, so Bella and Jack didn't get away until later this morning.

But, the additional hours had given her time to check on her Dad and to reassure herself that he was doing okay.

Nurse Marmie assured Bella that her Dad was healing as well as could be expected and that he would be fine for the week while her and Jack were on their honeymoon.

Bella glanced over at Jack who was busy working on his laptop.

Everyone believed they were enjoying a normal and relaxing honeymoon like all married couples in love.

It seemed both of them had been very convincing.

Even though Bella had enjoyed all the extra attention Jack showered on her during their wedding day yesterday, she knew it was only for show.

Nevertheless, when Jack had taken her to the Conservatory last night Bella's heart betrayed her. Her new husband's concern for her and the way he'd done his best to ease her stress, had reached into the deepest part of her heart. Later, when he'd surprised her by giving her the pink rose, she had all but melted.

That was the first time she'd glimpsed Jack's tender side.

Witnessing her husband's caring heart, caused Bella to hope that he was beginning to soften a little.

Yet, Jack's very business-like conversation with her this morning, dispelled that hope.

"We'll start by touring a couple of theme parks in Paris, then if we have time we'll take a look at those in the Netherlands. This should inspire us with fresh ideas so we can finish the designs for the Rose Adventure Park." Jack closed up his laptop computer, placed it inside its leather carrying case and turned toward her.

The plane taxied down the runway, finally coming to a stop.

"I've always wanted to see theme parks in Europe. This will be a great way to spark new ideas for theme park designs, but I hope we will also have fun." Bella held her purse tight to her chest as she stood to her feet.

Jack mumbled something about not wasting time and sticking to the project's deadline, as he walked behind her.

A limo was there to meet them and took them through the streets to their luxury hotel in the heart of the city. Jack put his hand on the small of her back as they walked through the columned entryway and into the spacious luxury hotel.

As they followed the concierge to the elevator, Bella couldn't help but notice the paintings of cherubs on the high ceilings.

To her it seemed like everything here was so grandiose with intricate designs like nothing she'd ever seen before. She could spend hours just looking at the artwork in this hotel alone.

"You'll be able to see more in the morning." Jack reached for her hand and Bella absentmindedly followed him still thinking of the beautiful designs.

The elevator took them to the top floor and their own private suite of rooms.

"Thank you." Jack gave the concierge a large tip after he brought their luggage into their suite and organized it in their rooms.

The glow of the lamp in the corner lit up the darkness, revealing a large suite with every possible convenience.

Jack walked to the middle of the room and looked around.

Bella held a hand to her mouth and stifled a yawn.

"I asked the concierge to put your bags in the bigger room." Jack pointed to the largest room on the south side.

A surge of relief swept over her. Jack had already planned out their separate rooms. She should've known he would. He was meticulous when it came to details.

Bella's cheeks warmed and she felt a little embarrassed at the direction of her thoughts. She peered up at him. "Thanks for organizing everything and for giving me the larger room Jack. That was thoughtful."

"Welcome." Jack stared at her for a moment, his expression unreadable. Bella squirmed under his intense gaze.

"Well, goodnight then." Bella nodded, hurrying toward the large bedroom sweeping the door closed.

She leaned her back against the door and expelled a breath.

Jack was far too appealing. He might have a scar on his face, but that didn't diminish his charm in any way. She would need to be extra vigilant to keep her heart from falling for her fake husband.

How would she manage to keep her distance when they were in close quarters for the next seven days?

BELLA HAD JUST STEPPED out of the shower the next morning when she heard a loud knock and someone calling out room service.

With hurried movements she fixed her hair, put on a little makeup and slipped into her comfy jeans and pink t-shirt.

As she stepped out of her room, she saw Jack sitting at the table drinking his coffee, busy working on his computer.

"Good morning." Bella walked toward the table where Jack sat. Room service had delivered a large breakfast that included orange juice and coffee.

The smell of bacon, eggs and hash browns wafted up her nose as she sat down at the table and her stomach growled loudly.

Jack glanced up at her. "Good morning. I take it you're hungry?" His grin was contagious as he set his computer aside and uncovered the food.

"Yeah. Famished actually." Reaching for the large spoon, she filled her plate.

Jack spoke of plans for the day in between bites. "I thought we could begin by going to one of the old book-shops here in Paris. Then after that we could visit one of the theme parks near the city."

"That would be lovely." Bella put down her orange juice a big smile on her face. "I'm excited to find some rare books."

"Good." He took a sip of his coffee and looked at his watch. "Pierre our driver, will have the car waiting below in fifteen minutes."

They both finished their breakfast around the same time, rode the elevator downstairs and hurried through the hotel's lobby.

"Morning Pierre. Thank you." Their driver held the door open for them and soon they drove slowly through the busy streets of Paris. The sounds of bicycle bells, scooters hurrying along and tires crunching over the cobbled streets were unique to the city of lights. It reminded Bella of 1950s noir films.

In the distance she spied the twelfth century Notre Dame cathedral and the Eiffel Tower that loomed tall over the city.

"If you like, we can come back to see more of the sights in Paris?" Jack's gaze caught her staring out the window at the sights.

"Yeah, that would be wonderful." Bella turned to Jack surprised that he would want to come back. She knew he was a man who liked to stay out of the limelight. It touched her that he would consider flying back to Paris so she could see more of the sights.

"But, for right now we'll see about finding rare books."

The driver slowed the car to a stop along a side street where there was less traffic. Jack stepped out onto the sidewalk holding her hand as they moved between the large crowds of people walking the sidewalks.

Jack held the door open to the large bookstore. The owners love of unique books was displayed in the store name, *Nous Aimons Les Livres Uniques,* which translated was *We Love Unique Books.*

Inside, there were upper and lower floors filled with books.

"*Bonjour* and welcome." The older gentleman welcomed them to his store.

"Hello." Bella greeted him and right away the man switched to English. "What can I help you find?"

"Do you have a section for rare books in English?" Bella asked.

"*Oui.* Of course. Follow me." The man took them up

the staircase to the second floor. "We have a lot of English speaking tourists so most of this upper floor is dedicated to English books. Anything I can help you find?"

"If you could show me where to find old science and historical books on inventions, that would be helpful."

"But, of course." The dignified older man, walked over to the far wall, where there were rows and rows of scientific books. "I hope you can find what you're looking for here."

"It looks great. We'll look through these books and see what we can find." Bella glanced up at the store owner and smiled. "Thank you so much."

"You're welcome. Let me know if you need anything else." He walked backed down the stairs.

Bella picked up a book on useful inventions for the home and started paging through it.

"Looking for a book for your Dad?" Jack turned to her, closing the book in his hand.

"Yes. He has often mentioned how he would like to read more about inventions in the eighteen hundreds or early nineteen hundreds. He thinks it would help his own creativity and inspire new designs."

"He's probably right." Jack set down his book and picked up another browsing through its pages.

Bella was too aware of Jack standing next to her as she skimmed through the text of an old book.

The scent of sandalwood and a fresh outdoorsy smell she loved so much, wafted up her nose as she stood close to her new husband.

Peering up at him, she admired his handsome face as well as the fact that Jack took her to a bookstore, knowing that she loved it so much. A tuft of brown hair slipped down over one eyebrow and she had to stop herself from reaching up to push the curl back in place.

Jack turned his head suddenly and her cheeks heated as his gaze met hers.

Embarrassed to be caught staring, she showed him the hand drawn picture in the yellowed pages. "This book would be something Dad would find interesting."

"I think you're right." He leaned closer and whispered, "But personally I find the woman next to me, far more intriguing than a history book on science."

The corners of her mouth turned up at his compliment and Bella turned to look at him. As soon as she did, she realized her mistake. Jack's face was so close to her own that she could feel his warm breath on her skin. His lips were mere inches from hers.

Bella peered up to see Jack's hazel eyes darken with intensity. She moistened her lips with the tip of her tongue her thoughts all in a tangle from his compliment.

Jack leaned down, his eyes focused on her lips, when the bell attached to the front door chimed announcing more visitors to the bookstore.

Bella hurriedly stepped away from Jack. His lips formed a slow grin as if enjoying every moment of her discomfort.

She dropped the book in her hand and reached down to put it in the basket, telling herself she would not let Jack fluster her.

"I'm going to look at a few more books before we go." Bella was desperate to move away from Jack.

"Take your time." The sound of his lazy voice irritated

her. Why wasn't he flustered like she was? He almost kissed her in a public bookstore.

Bella swallowed trying to clear away her frustration and walked to the next aisle. It took a few minutes to calm her nerves before she could focus on books some of her clients had asked for through her website. She didn't know how long she took looking through the book shelves among the aisles, but she did her best to get two of every book. That way she would have books in stock for the next person.

With her basket full, she looked along the aisles until she found Jack.

"Did you find the books you were looking for?" Jack grinned at the sight of books that were beginning to over-flow her basket.

"Yes. I was happy to find a few of the books my website customers needed. I also found what looks to be a really old version of the novel, *Pride and Prejudice* by Jane Austen."

"Where did you see it?"

Bella walked over to the aisle. "I don't know if it's a first edition of the book, but I found it here." Bella looked along the bookshelf and under other books, her brow furrowed. "That's strange. The book was here just a minute ago."

Jack looked along the shelf. "Hmm, I don't see it here either. I'll ask the storeowner if he knows where it would have gone to."

"That's a good idea."

Jack reached over and took the heavy basket from her hands. "Looks like we're ready to go then."

"Yes we are. Thanks Jack." Bella had a big grin on her face as she walked down the stairs. She was so excited about all the great books she'd found.

Jack bought the books and asked for sturdy canvas bags. They left the store and found Pierre waiting for them. Soon they were on their way.

The driver let them off at the front entrance to one of the most popular theme parks in Paris.

A large pink castle dominated one end of the theme park with the hidden dragon lurking beneath it. A massive mountain with a roller coaster ride, looked inviting. Jack bought their pass and they walked into the park.

"Oh Jack. Let's take a picture with these characters." Bella saw seven dwarf-like characters all dressed up as miners. She grabbed Jack's hand, pulling him over to join the line up of other picture-takers.

"Bella, I don't like to get my picture taken."

"Oh Jack, just this once?"

Jack nodded, a small resigned smile on his face.

"Put your arm around your wife and stand close together." The photographer spoke to Jack. He complied and placed his arm around her, pulling her close to his side.

Warm tingles ran down her back and arms where Jack touched her. He kissed the top of her head and the photographer started snapping his camera. The dwarves surrounded them on both sides.

It wasn't long before the photographer finished.

"Do you want them all or only a few?"

"We'll take them all." Jack paid the man and his assistant sent access to all the pictures through email.

Bella beamed up at him. "Thank you Jack."

Together they walked toward the massive mountain with it's underground roller coaster. They had to wait in the queue for a few minutes.

Laughter and screams filled the air around them.

"Sounds like people are having fun." Bella got out her smartphone, opened the note taking app and started typing.

"What are you doing?" Jack lifted one eyebrow studying her.

"I'm taking notes on how we feel about each ride and what people around us are saying about the rides we go on. That way we'll have a better feel for what people are really excited about as we design the adventure park." Bella was busy writing down what the teenagers ahead of them said about what they didn't like about their last ride. "I want to write it down in their words, and speak their language. That will help us when we're ready to market the Adventure Park to the public."

"Impressive." Jack looked at her as if seeing her for the first time.

Bella warmed at his praise. "Just doing what I need to do to get a good feel for what people love in a theme park."

Before long it was their turn to get on the roller coaster. They sat down in the blue cone-shaped rocket. Bella sat in the seat in front of Jack, making some last notes on her smartphone.

"Hang on Bella. Here we go." Bella quickly slipped her smartphone in her pocket. As the cone shaped rocket propelled forward she gripped the handles in front of her.

They rode the rails and the pulsating blue lights got faster as the went. After many twists and turns travelling through the field of stars, comets, asteroids and a red swirling wormhole, they finally slowed down as they reached the unloading station.

Jack jumped off first and held his hand out. Bella put her hand in his, throwing him a shaky smile. Her legs wobbled as she stepped out and Jack put his arm around her waist.

"You okay?" His warm breath against her ear sent shivers up her spine.

"Yeah, I'm okay. Just a little shook up from flying at the speed of light through space." Bella grinned at him. When one corner of his mouth turned up it felt like a win as Jack didn't smile as much as he should.

"Do you want to stop? We could just walk around the park." They stepped outside once again. Bella closed her eyes for a moment enjoying the heat of the sun on her skin.

"No, we don't need to stop Jack. I'm okay." She peered up at him with a grin.

"Well we really only have time to see two more items on our list. Should we tour the sleeping princess's castle and check out the Pirate ship?"

Bella grinned and grabbed his hand. "Sounds like fun."

Jack squeezed her hand and they began walking. He stopped and bought two bottles of water to take with them.

It was enchanting to walk across the drawbridge and under the archway of the castle. They began to follow along with the fairy-tale as they walked.

Bella got a closer look at the stained glass castle windows. Each window was a beautiful illustration of each part of the love story between the princess and her prince.

They walked all the way through to the last station where the storybook and vivid images portrayed true love's first kiss.

Bella sighed at the romantic ending and looked up at Jack.

Jack raised his eyebrows and looked at the ceiling as they walked out of the castle. "I guess for a fairy-tale love story it is pretty good." He pointed back to the castle. "But, we all know that's definitely not real life."

Bella sighed to herself. She'd only heard small tidbits of Jack's marriage and the death of his wife and unborn son from Aunt Maisie. Even though she didn't know all the details, she could tell Jack was hurting.

It was clear he was cynical about love.

She hoped that someday Jack would be able to let go of that pain and heartache.

The Pirates sign loomed over their heads and they stepped into the cave-like building where they would ride in the Pirate ship. Palm trees hung down from their tall perches and bony skeletons dangled in the corners.

As they passed by another ride, she noticed one man with red hair and beard who had an uncanny resemblance to the man who grabbed her from the street all those years ago.

Bella stopped and her whole body shuddered. The man turned toward her. When she realized it wasn't the same man, she breathed out slowly.

"What's wrong?" Jack put his hand under her chin and looked into her eyes.

"Oh nothing." Bella exhaled an unsteady breath. "I think I'm seeing things. Here in this darkened cave the shadows are somewhat unnerving."

He arched one brow, looking doubtfully at her before they walked toward the next ride.

They showed their pass to the teenager at the entrance and they soon were seated side-by-side in the front row of the pirate ship.

As the ship moved along the water, the rippling sound of moving water was soothing to Bella's rattled nerves.

"Now this is fun. The design I had in mind for the pirate ship at the *Rose Adventure Park* looks a little more adventurous. But this is also quite diverting." Jack pointed to the man swinging from a rope across the water. They turned a corner and suddenly there were pirates and booty everywhere on the small island beside the water.

It was too dark to take notes. Bella made a mental note to remember all the details so she could write them down later.

The ship continued to move forward going down a small waterfall and then toward a long dark cave. Bella grabbed Jack's hand as they went inside the cave, her hands clammy with fear.

Without warning, the ship stopped in the middle of the cave. It was pitch black all around them.

"Jack why did we stop?"

"I don't know. I'm sure we'll be moving again soon."

A man behind them got out of the boat to go contact the theme park's manager, to tell them what happened.

Bella's teeth chattered and her knees started shaking. "I'm scared Jack."

"Come here. I'm right beside you. I'll take care of you." Jack put his arm around her and pulled her close. Bella leaned her head on his chest and put her arms around his waist, needing to feel his warmth and protection.

"I just don't like dark places. It makes me feel trapped. Being in this dark cave feels a lot like that. I'm really worried." Bella chattered on, her fears getting the better of her.

"Maybe I can help."

"How can you…" Bella whispered, when suddenly she felt Jack's hand tilt her chin upwards. His lips touched down on hers.

Bella shivered as the warmth of his lips caressed hers. Melting into his embrace she slid her arms around his neck, drawing him closer.

Her husband's hands moved in soft circles along her back. His lips nipped and pulled on her own. Her body melted in a liquid pool of heat with his sweet kiss. She never wanted it to end.

Suddenly, a loud rumbling noise began beneath the boat.

Startled, Bella pulled away. "The boat is moving again."

"Good." Jack spoke, his voice sounding out of breath as he removed his arm from around her.

Bella thought she heard him mumble something about the motor starting not a moment too soon, but it was hard to hear with the noise of people talking and the whirring of the boat.

The boat moved out of the dark cave and into the sunlight.

Bella's face heated as she thought of Jack's kisses. Her lips still throbbed from his tender exploration. He was probably right that it wasn't a moment too soon that the motor turned on because she could have kissed him all night long.

Her feelings for him were getting more confusing with each day she spent time with him. Bella peered over at him, only to see him studying her, his brows furrowed.

"What's wrong?"

"Nothing's wrong. Not a blasted thing." Jack words were short, his voice sounding gruff.

Bella squared her shoulders and looked straight ahead, ignoring his surliness.

Jack was confusing, not to mention maddening.

One moment he was kind and thoughtful and the next moment he acted like a surly beast. One moment he kissed her like he was starved for his last meal and the next moment he was gruff and bad mannered.

She reminded herself of the terms of their marriage contract.

Their agreement was for a marriage-in-name-only. Falling in love with him was not part of the plan.

Bella was determined not to let a few of Jack's kisses turn her head. She just needed to keep her distance.

How would she do that, when she was endlessly fascinated by him?

They had been forced together for days on end. How would she manage to avoid getting closer to him?

CHAPTER EIGHT

ack

CLOSING the door to their hotel suite Jack leaned his head against the solid wood and expelled a slow breath.

His gaze followed Bella who walked to the small kitchenette.

Jack walked behind her, guilt causing him to stumble a little as he followed.

He needed to apologize.

She turned on the faucet, pouring water into a glass.

"Bella, I'm sorry for being rude earlier." Jack leaned a hip against the table. He stared at the back of her head willing her to turn around and look at him.

She stood motionless for a moment, the cup in her hand shaking a little before she turned slowly to face him.

"I don't understand why you're in a good mood one minute and all in a temper the next."

"I know and I apologize." Jack rubbed the back of his neck and grimaced. "I'm sorry for taking my frustration out on you. You don't deserve that."

Jack wanted to tell his new wife that she made him crazy. Bella's sweet kisses had stirred a desire in him that caused him to want her more than he should.

He couldn't remember ever feeling this strongly for a woman before. Not even Elin had made him feel like this.

Awareness unfolded inside him. He was frustrated because his traitorous heart was doing the very thing he'd told it not to do… fall for his fake wife.

The passion he had for Bella was unexpected and alarming — feelings he was very afraid were only growing stronger.

Jack was convinced if he told Bella any of this it would shock her just like it shook him to his core right now. His brows puckered together in deep thought, uncertain of what to tell her.

Bella stood close to him, her brown hair a little mussed from the wind and her big brown eyes gazing into his.

A slight smile formed and she reached over, softly touching his hand. "Thanks for apologizing. I forgive you." Bella paused and pulled her hand back. She studied him while her hands fidgeted nervously.

Seeing his wife's unease Jack decided this was the perfect time to give her his gift. "I have something to give you that I hope will cheer you."

"Jack you really didn't need to get me anything." Bella bit her bottom lip slowly.

Jack walked over to where he'd hid the wrapped package and handed it to her.

Bella smiled slightly as she opened up the beautifully wrapped gift. Her eyes widened and her jaw dropped in surprise.

Covering her lips with one hand she sighed in wonder with what he'd given her. "You bought me a first edition of *Pride and Prejudice*." Tears filled her eyes and she quickly wiped them away. "Oh my goodness, Jack. I've wanted this rare book since I was a little girl." She lovingly touched the yellowed pages. "I don't even know what to say. Thank you seems so inadequate. But, thank you so very much."

"You're welcome Bella. I'm just happy to see your smile again."

His wife held the book to her chest and stepped closer to him. She stood on tiptoe, placing a light kiss on the right side of his face right where the scar was and whispered in his ear. "This is the best day ever." Bella stepped away from him a shimmer of tears in her big brown eyes. Jack felt a sudden sense of loss as she moved away.

She hesitated for a moment before she whispered. "Goodnight."

As she closed the door to her bedroom, he touched one hand to his cheek still feeling the warmth of her lips on his skin. He'd nearly melted when his wife touched him. He'd wanted to pull her into his arms again, but that's where the trouble today had started.

When it came to Bella, he needed to leave well enough alone.

Confusion and frustration filled him. His fake wife had him all tied up in knots. Did she even realize she'd kissed the right side of his face with all it's imperfections? Maybe it really didn't matter to her and she accepted him just as he was...

Jack ran a hand through his hair, his thoughts consumed by Bella as he entered his bedroom. Lying down on his bed, his mind returned to his wife. He loved her carefree laughter, her gentleness and her sweet kisses.

Hours later, he finally fell asleep only to be awakened suddenly in the middle of the night.

Loud screams came from the other room.

Jack scrambled out of bed rushing to Bella's bedroom.

"No! Don't take me. Let me go. Please, let me out of here!" Bella cried out. Her face was contorted in pain and tears ran down her cheeks.

His wife's wild thrashing back and forth mingled with her loud cries caused knots to form in his stomach. He hurried to her side, sat down on the bed and pulled her into his arms.

"Shh, sweetheart. You'll be okay. I've got you. You're safe now." Jack kissed the top of her head and whispered softly, hoping to calm her.

Her eyes opened and her body stiffened in his arms as she stared at him wide-eyed. "Jack?"

"It's okay, I'm here. You were having a nightmare. I'll stay with you until you get back to sleep." He spoke softly not wanting to alarm her any further.

Bella relaxed a little in his arms, rubbing the tears from her eyes.

Jack whispered softly, "Would it help to talk about it?"

"Ah... no. Well, maybe." She pushed herself up and

leaned her head against his shoulder. With one hand she rubbed her forehead.

Jack reached for her other hand and rubbed soothing circles with his thumb. "Tell me Bella. Maybe if you talked about your bad dream it would help you get back to sleep."

Regret clouded his thoughts. He'd done a poor job of making his wife feel safe and protected. He hoped by listening and being at her side, Bella would start to open up again.

"I'm fairly certain this bad dream occurred because I saw a guy yesterday who looked similar to the kidnapper." Bella shivered. "It was the same recurring nightmare I've had ever since those awful men kidnapped me in high school."

Looking up at him she hesitated. "But I'm not sure if I should tell you, because after you saved me that day and I gushed my gratitude, you told me you never wanted to hear me talk about it again."

Memories came flooding back to him of the day he had chased the man who was dragging Bella to his van. The kidnapper had already pushed her inside the van, when Jack came up behind him and roughed him up. The perp had sliced Jack's cheek as he was taking Bella out of the van.

Jack kicked him again so that he was down for the count, before he ran off with Bella at his side. Once they were safe, Bella had given him her handkerchief and cried a heartfelt thank you over and over again.

He had pressed the handkerchief against his cheek to

stop the flow of blood and he remembered telling Bella that he never wanted to talk about what happened again.

Remembering his harsh words that day, sudden remorse rushed through him. "I'm so sorry, Bella. Can you forgive me for being so callous of your feelings?" Jack released a long slow breath. "If you're willing to talk about it now, I'm listening."

Bella pulled her knees up to her chest, her chin resting there before she turned to look at him. "Thank you for saying that. And it's okay, I forgive you Jack."

She pulled the blanket up over her legs. Jack was glad she did. The kittens on her pyjama t-shirt and shorts and her long legs were very appealing and it made it difficult for him to focus on what she was saying.

Taking a deep breath, she began. "All right, here goes. My nightmare is always the same. I'm back at the High School Science fair with my Dad and we're in a strange city. Elle is with me and once again we're walking back to our hotel. This time in the dream, Elle gets away, but I'm kidnapped and gagged with my hands bound and thrown into a van. I hear you calling my name but the kidnapper gets in the van and drives away. I look out the window and see you running after the van, but it's too late. I'm trapped and forever lost from my family and friends."

She pressed her head against her knees, shoulders shaking with sobs as she relived the terror of her nightmare.

Jack picked Bella up and with gentle movements placed her on his lap. With one hand he pulled her quivering body close and with the other he stroked her head gently.

"Shh, sweetheart. You're safe here with me. I've got you." Jack kissed the top of her head, frustrated at how helpless he was to take away her tears.

Closing his eyes he sighed deeply as he thought about Bella's words. He'd been so caught up in himself and his own problems back then, that he hadn't been aware of just how much trauma she lived through. "I never realized just how terrifying that must have been for you. I'm sorry."

"It's not your fault. You didn't know." Bella wiped away her tears with the back of her hand and snuggled against him.

Jack shifted on the bed, an increased desire for his new wife making him uncomfortable as he held her close.

"Will you stay with me Jack? I'm too scared to be alone tonight." Her whispered plea flooded him with compassion. He wondered just how deep the wounds were from when she was kidnapped.

"I'll stay beside you. I promise." As he held Bella close to his heart, a fierce protectiveness overtook him. Anger surged through him at the thought of anyone trying to hurt his wife again.

Slowly her tears subsided to whimpers and soon silence filled the room except for the sound of Bella's even breathing.

She had fallen asleep.

Jack held her for a while longer, enjoying the flowery scent of her hair as he held her soft body next to his.

Looking down, he stared at the perfect shape of her face, her smooth, unmarred skin a reflection of the pure beauty within her.

He kissed her forehead as she lay still against his chest.

Jack's heart rate accelerated just being close to her.

He expelled a slow breath. What was happening to him? It scared him that he was beginning to like her a little too much. The way he longed to see her smile and to feel her touch surprised and terrified him at the same time.

Repeatedly he warned himself not to get too close or fall in love with another woman again after the terrible marriage with his first wife. That had been a huge mistake and he wasn't going to make another one like it.

Yet, he realized Bella was so completely different than Elin. Bella was kind, generous and someone who didn't seem to worry overmuch about appearances and how she looked to others.

His wife had a kindness about her, which spread to everything she did and everyone she knew. Everyone she talked to went away feeling better about themselves. Lately, Jack found himself finding reasons to be by her side.

This new awareness and longing to be with Bella scared him. Jack was starting to like her a little too much.

Falling for his fake wife was a luxury he couldn't afford.

He loosened her arms around his waist, placed her down on the bed and covered her with a blanket.

Jack lay down beside her and pulled her into his arms. He wanted to kiss her and if he were honest, he wanted much more than that. Dragging his thoughts away from temptation, he circled his thoughts back to all Bella had told him.

An unexplainable desire rose inside Jack to do whatever he needed to do to protect his wife from any more pain or heartache. She'd been through so much.

But, how could he protect her and stop his own heart from falling for her in the process?

Jack realized what he really needed to do was to put distance between him and Bella. He had no idea how he'd do that, but the fear of loving and being pushed away again was too strong to ignore.

He would need to keep his heart well shielded from pain.

§

BELLA OPENED her eyes the next morning, groggy from a restless sleep.

The weight of the blanket was too heavy. When she started to move it off, she found Jack's hand on her waist. She caught her breath and closed her eyes for a moment. Vague impressions from the night before skittered across her mind.

She'd thought it was just a dream.

His warm breath tickled her neck, reminding her that her fake husband in her bed was indeed very real.

The nightmare must have returned and Jack had come to her room to calm her down.

Heat began in her neck and climbed up her cheeks.

She was mortified that Jack had seen her at her most vulnerable, right after one of her nightmares.

With slow movements she lifted his hand off her waist, got out from under the covers and grabbed jeans and a t-shirt.

Hurrying to get dressed, she tiptoed to the kitchen to make coffee.

As she put the coffee grounds in the coffee maker, she rubbed her forehead, agitated about the night before. Memories of Jack pulling her onto his lap and how he held her in a close embrace made her yearn for more.

Warm tingles formed in her belly as she remembered how his hands ran soft circles along her back. His sweet words made her feel cared for and loved.

Her hand shook slightly as she poured cream in her coffee cup. The realization hit her that she was beginning to fall for Jack.

Bella couldn't let that happen.

She wouldn't let herself be trapped by falling in love with her fake husband. Bella had experienced what it was like to feel powerless when she dated Mason in high school and then again when she was kidnapped. She was convinced that if she fell in love, she would no longer have the freedom and independence she craved.

Bella reminded herself that all she needed was to make sure that she completed her father's contract, that her Dad got the medical care he needed to get better and that she was able to pay off their debt. Those were the most important things.

Falling in love with Jack would take away her independence and force her to give up her goals and dreams.

Bella couldn't let that happen.

She picked up her mug of coffee and walked toward the kitchen table, doing her best to think about something other than Jack.

"You look well rested, even after waking up in the

middle of the night." Jack leaned against the doorpost watching her.

Bella spilled her coffee at the sound of his deep voice. Looking up she saw him leaning against the door frame of his bedroom, his intense gaze riveted on her.

"About last night…" Bella began, when Jack interrupted her.

"Bella, don't worry about it. You had a nightmare, it happens." Jack took the napkins out of her hand and squatted down to wipe up the coffee spill.

It seemed to her like Jack didn't want to talk about last night. Well, that was fine with her. She was scared to be even more vulnerable with Jack. If she let him get too close, it would be much too easy to lose the freedom she craved.

"Thanks, Jack."

He tossed the napkins in the garbage, poured himself a cup of coffee and turned to her, his pirate smile in place. "No problem. So are you ready to look at another theme park today?"

At her nod, Jack set his coffee on the table, pulled out his laptop and started searching for something online.

"Sure." Bella really wanted to ask him what she had said in her half asleep, half conscious state last night. But, if his swift change of subject and the disinterested look on his face were any indication, Bella decided she would be wise to leave well enough alone for now.

"What do you think about going to the Netherlands?" He turned his laptop around to show her the screen.

Bella scanned the website of the largest theme park in the Netherlands. She was especially interested in the fairy-tale theme forest. As she clicked on the different attractions like Rapunzel, Sleeping Beauty and Hansel and Gretel, her interest heightened.

"I adore the fairy-tale theme forest with the different houses and figures they created to represent interesting creatures. Kids must love this." Bella looked up at Jack, a huge grin on her face. "When do we leave?"

"I thought we could go shopping for some designer clothes for you this morning and then we'll fly out in the afternoon. Our driver will be here in one hour."

"Clothes for me?"

"Yes. I noticed that you could use more, so I thought we'd go to the Avenue des Champs-Elysées which has some of the most popular designer clothing in Paris."

Bella nervously stood to her feet, intimidated at the thought of going to the most luxurious clothing stores in the city. But, she knew it was important that she have clothes that would make Jack proud to have her by his side at benefit galas and other events.

"All right. I'll go have a shower and get ready, then." She stood, grinned at Jack and hurried to her room excited to try on new clothes and to visit the new adventure park.

JACK COULDN'T HELP but smile to himself.

Bella wore her heart on her sleeve, which meant most of the time there was no doubt about how she felt about anything.

Sometimes, that part of her personality was difficult to resist.

When he first saw her walking with her head hung down toward the kitchen table, he had to stop himself from walking over and wrapping his arms around her.

Jack wanted to hear what she had to say and to comfort her, but he couldn't let himself get more attached to her than he already was.

Bella was his fake wife. She was with him for now, but would be gone at the end of one year.

Lately, he needed to remind himself daily that this was a marriage-in-name-only.

It would be far too easy to forget, when faced everyday with Bella's captivating beauty and inviting smile.

As he closed his laptop and slipped it inside the case, he admitted to himself there was another reason he had interrupted Bella before.

He didn't want to get too close to Bella, listening to her most intimate thoughts, or her hearing his. If he got too close, she would realize the horrible truth.

That he wasn't worthy to be her husband.

Jack squashed the stabbing pain that pierced him at the thought of Bella seeing him as he really was -- beastly. He hurried to his feet to get away from the terrible truth about himself.

He packed his suitcase in a hurry stuffing down his feelings, much like he hid his clothes in his satchel. Carrying it to the door, it wasn't long before Bella joined him. The concierge took their suitcases and they went down the elevator to their waiting car.

Soon the driver took them to the beautiful boulevard

and they began by shopping at Louis Vuitton. Bella was amazed at the prices. One dress cost two months wages.

The women in the stores began finding clothes for Bella and it seemed Jack had decided to see what he thought looked good on her.

"The short sleeved black dress with the tiny gold buttons looks great. We'll take it as well as the matching shoes and the black handbag with gold detailing." Jack sat in a chair in the private changing area and would nod or shake his head as Bella showed him different clothes she tried on.

By the time they finished shopping near lunchtime, they had also gone to five different well-known designer clothing stores.

After they finally finished shopping, Jack took Bella to a small cafe that overlooked the Seine river. The few times he had visited Paris, this had been a favorite cafe to relax and eat.

The waiter led them to the outside patio that over-looked the river. Ordering a light meal, they enjoyed sitting in the sun.

"Jack, I appreciate you taking me to all those luxury stores. And thank you for so many amazing clothes and accessories. Everything is beautiful. I still think you bought me too much, but I do thank you." Bella took a sip of her lemon water, smiling over at him.

"Bella it wasn't too much. You needed everything we bought. And I was happy to do it." Jack cocked his head to one side, still marvelling at the fact that his wife was telling him he shouldn't have bought so many clothes for her. That was the first time he'd heard any woman tell him that.

A faint memory came back of his first wife telling him to double her clothing budget each month. He'd always been very generous, but he also wanted them to be wise with their money — a habit that had been drilled into him by his Dad as a small boy.

However, as it turned out, even doubling her clothing budget still hadn't made his first wife happy. So he'd become somewhat cynical about women and felt like their real motives were hidden and that he couldn't trust most of them.

Bella was so different from any woman he'd ever known. It was a pleasure to buy things for her because she was always grateful. She also didn't try to take advantage of him.

Jack had begun to feel like he could trust his wife. He was happy she liked her new clothes. The beep of his smart-phone showed a text from their driver. "Looks like Pierre is on his way. The stores have delivered your packages. Next stop, the Netherlands." Jack smiled at Bella's huge grin.

"I'm looking forward to it Jack." They walked out of the cafe and drove to the airport.

Not long after they were seated in the airplane, Bella fell asleep. It was only when the captain announced that they would soon be landing, that she woke up. The next hour was a flurry of activity. They went to the hotel and dropped the suitcases and packages off there.

Bella changed into her new deep green designer Capri pants and yellow and green matching short-sleeved top.

Jack's hazel eyes darkened in appreciation as she walked toward him. Everything she wore looked beautiful on her.

Bella smiled and Jack's whole world lit up. That feeling lingered on their walk through the theme park.

"It might be good if we had more interesting things for little children at the Adventure Park." Jack sat across from Bella in a teacup ride, his arms stretched out on the back of the bench chair that moved them up and down in a circular motion.

"You're right. And the little children would attract more parents and grandparents to the park." Bella had her smartphone out and was busy jotting down ideas.

After the ride, together they walked through the fairy-tale themed forest.

Bella's eyes lit up as they passed the candy house of Hansel and Gretel. "It actually smells like vanilla cake here." Her nose twitched and her lilting laugh and wide smile was contagious.

"Hmm, now I'm hungry." Many enchanting attractions caught their eye: A statue of Little Red Riding Hood, a talking tree and a character whose head was much taller than the rest of his body. Jack lifted one eyebrow at the very interesting characters in the fairy-tale themed forest.

As the day drew to a close, they went on a roller coaster ride that took them over the water rapids and ended with a big spray of water.

"It's a good thing this is the last ride of the day." Bella giggled taking in his wet shirt and her own soaked clothes.

He gripped her waist, lifting her out of the boat. As her

body pressed against his own, it was the sweetest torture he'd ever known to have Bella move into his waiting arms. Her soft feminine body molded against his, her arms curling around his neck as she slid smoothly to the ground.

He wanted to breathe in deeply of her flowery scent. He wanted to kiss her sweet lips. He wanted to hold onto her forever.

Bella's upturned face was beautiful and enticing, and for a moment he nearly gave into the impulse to forget his decision to keep his distance.

As difficult as it was, Jack forced himself to remove his hands from her waist. He stepped away from her.

For a moment Bella stared at him, her smile gone as she studied him. Then she blinked, her smiled forced as she took a tiny step away from him. "Ready to go?"

Jack nodded, guilt gnawing at him for causing his wife any hurt. He saw an uneasiness in the stiffness of her shoulders.

He held out his arm, but Bella wasn't taking him up on his offer. Walking together toward the exit, they kept their communication to polite responses and smiles.

Jack sighed realizing too late, that by forcing himself to keep his distance from his fake wife, he'd caused a wedge between them.

CHAPTER NINE

ella

"Rory, I'm scared of my own weakness when it comes to Jack." Bella sat across from her friend in the corner of Betty's Cafe, and sipped her coffee.

Bella had texted Rory yesterday, desperately needing the listening ear of a friend.

It had been four days since they'd flown back from Europe, and Jack had been working every day late into the evening on designs for clients. He'd also been busy organizing the workers he'd hired to work the Silver Mine he'd just inherited from his great-grandfather.

Except for those few minutes that Jack took each day to go over design ideas with Bella for the Adventure Park, she hadn't seen him much.

After a week of getting closer, they had now retreated from each other.

"What do you mean?" Rory took a small bite of her muffin, using her napkin to delicately wipe away crumbs from her mouth.

"Well, the week we had together in Europe went far better than I expected." Bella let out a heavy sigh. "And now I find that I'm attracted to Jack a lot more than I should be."

Bella set down her coffee mug, her fingers toying absently with the spoon beside her plate.

"Hmm, it sounds like you've been thoroughly wooed and kissed by your husband. That's truly horrible." Rory touched the back of her hand to her forehead in a dramatic woe-is-me-sigh.

"Fake husband." To Bella's mind, those two words made all the difference.

Rory shook her head slightly and relaxed back in her chair. "Okay, tell me. What is it exactly about your relationship with Jack that's got you so worried?"

"Well, he treated me like a princess during our trip. He spent time with me, bought me clothes and even took me to a rare bookstore where he bought me a first edition of Jane Austen's *Pride and Prejudice* novel." Bella looked out the window, heat rising in her neck and cheeks as more memories surfaced.

"Then, one night I had another one of my nightmares. Jack held me and comforted me until I was calm enough to fall back asleep. Now that he's had a deeper glimpse into my heart, we've become much closer. To be honest, it terrified me so much I started to back away from him."

Bella's lips formed into a thin line, her brows puckered in worry.

Rory leaned forward, her elbows on the table, her gaze unflinching. "Bella, listen to me. I know you're scared. Heaven knows, I would be too if I were in your shoes. But, I really think you need to give Jack a chance. You said he's been good to you. Why not see where this relationship goes?"

"Because that's not how *this* relationship is supposed to go. Jack and I agreed on a fake marriage, not a real one." Bella's voice started to break and stress lines appeared around her eyes. "We're supposed to stay married as friends for one year only and then get a quiet divorce. This fake marriage is supposed to be effortless and well-controlled. There's supposed to be no hurt feelings in the end."

Rory laughed and shook her head. "You make this sound like a science experiment Bella. Since when is any relationship effortless and well-controlled?"

Bella shrugged, realizing the truth of Rory's words. "Okay, you're right. Relationships are complicated. But, that's the part that worries me. How will I be able to put a stop to this attraction to Jack and get through the next eleven months without making a fool of myself?"

"Do you need to put a stop to it, Bella? You said yourself that Jack treated you like a princess during your honeymoon. Maybe you're not the only one who is struggling with their feelings. What if Jack is falling for you?" Rory studied her and a satisfied smile turned her lips upward as her hands rested under her chin.

She opened her mouth and shut it a few times before

speaking, remembering their week together. "No, I don't think so." Bella remembered his passionate kisses, but she also remembered how he'd pulled away from her on their last day together. By the time they'd flown home, Jack had already put a whole lot of distance between them.

"Why would you say that? Sounds like Jack has been passionately wooing you."

Bella breathed out a heavy sigh. "I'm not sure. Sometimes it seems like he's wooing me, but then the next day he puts giant walls between us. He's been giving me too many mixed signals."

Rory leaned closer to Bella, her eyes pinning her to the spot in a laser-like focus. "Is it possible the two of you have given each other mixed signals? It seems to me, you two just need to stop avoiding each other and see where your relationship goes."

"He's so busy."

"You live in the same house, Bella. You're designing a project together. Talk to Jack." Rory leaned closer, her eyes focused on hers like a laser beam.

"You're right. I need to stop letting fear hold me back." Bella nodded almost to herself. "I'll talk to him."

All too soon, it was time for them to leave. Rory left the coffee shop with her three Aunts and Bella went home to work on the finishing touches of the latest design for the adventure park.

Driving up the hill, she wondered if Jack would be home or if he was working late at his office down the hill. As she drove her vehicle through the gates she saw Jack's truck parked in front of the garage.

Sighing, she parked beside his truck. Carrying the heavy bags, she walked into the house.

"I'll carry those to your office." Ben was waiting at the door when she arrived.

"Thanks Ben." He walked down the hall to her office. Bella was about to follow when she heard her Dad's voice coming from the kitchen.

She hung up her coat and walked toward the kitchen, smiling as she heard Chipper talking with her father.

"Chipper, do you think your Grandma will let me snatch one of her cookies?" Her Dad's voice could be heard clearly, above the whirring of the mixer in the background. Bella stepped into the kitchen, greeted by the heavenly scent of chocolate chip cookies. Mrs. Potter turned around to stick the next pan of cookies into oven.

"She won't mind. Grandma lets me have a snack after I've done my chores for the day. Did you finish your chores Mr. Campbell?" Chipper at ten years old, had a personality that suited his name. He was always found helping Mrs. Potter carry this and that everyday after school.

"Well, lately I haven't had that many chores, so I guess I'm finished my chores for the day." Her Dad winked at him.

"In that case, here you go." Chipper handed a cookie into her Dad's eager hand.

"Hi Dad." Bella was greeted by her Dad's wide smile, which always made her feel so loved. She walked over to him and gave him a big hug, whispering in his ear. "What does your nurse say about eating cookies?"

"Ah Beauty, I'm happy to see you." Her Dad turned at

the sound of her voice and put his arm around her, sighing, "I know. I'm not to have too many sweets, but maybe one will be okay."

Bella kissed his cheek. "Okay."

"Dunlin Campbell, I saw that." Nurse Marmie walked into the kitchen and put her hands on her hips. The corners of her mouth turned up as she silently stared at her patient and shook her head.

"Ah, it's only one cookie, lass. Surely you'll not deny me this wee bit of pleasure?" Dunlin winked at his nurse and grinned.

"Oh I suppose just this once wouldn't hurt." Glancing at her Dad's nurse, Bella noticed a telltale blush creeping up her neck and onto her cheeks.

Nurse Marmie's normal composure slipped a little with her Dad's charm. It made her wonder if there was more going on between them than she realized.

It had always been just Bella and her Dad. As she studied the two of them, it suddenly dawned on her that maybe now that her father saw his only daughter married, maybe he was open to the idea of marrying again. It was possible that soon she would need to share his affections.

Insecurity tugged at her with the new changes going on around her.

"Since you're in good hands Dad, I'll get going." Bella started to turn, but the housekeeper stopped her in her tracks.

"Bella, before you leave have a cookie." Mrs. Potter smiled at her pushing the pan of fresh cookies her way. "You need to put some fat on those bones."

She laughed at her grandmotherly concern. "Mrs.

Potter, I couldn't possibly. I'm still too full from lunch. Maybe I'll stop by later and grab one then, if that's okay by you?"

"Most likely later on, you'll be busy talking to our Jack. He was here not thirty minutes ago asking where you were." Mrs. Potter leaned over and whispered. "If you ask me, he seemed a little hot under the collar that you weren't here."

"Oh. I'll check to see if Jack's in his office." Bella's voice came out wobbly and unsure. She tossed a quick smile, kissed her father's cheek and hurried out of the kitchen.

Bella walked down the hallway just past the library, and knocked softly on Jack's office door. There was no answer, so she went to her office across the hall thinking she would get started on the new designs before Jack came back.

She had just opened the design software to the project when Jack burst into the room. "Here you are." He closed the door and walked over to her desk, sounding out of breath. "I've been looking all over for you. Where have you been?"

Jack walked around the desk and leaned a hip against her desk. His arms were folded across his chest as he waited for an answer. His expression was cool and detached as he stared at her.

Bella's shoulders tensed, bracing herself. She really didn't want to fight with him, but he was making it really difficult for her not to be on the defensive.

Maybe he'd calm down if she explained. "I went to Betty's Cafe to eat lunch with Rory. I thought you would be gone all day, so I didn't leave a note. I didn't mean to worry you."

Jack's shoulders relaxed a little and he rubbed his chin.

Bella's forehead furrowed and she wondered what was going on with Jack. Why would he feel so worried about her leaving?

He sat on the edge of her desk, toying with her colored pens, before looking her way again. As much as his question and cool manner frustrated her, she couldn't help but sense there was a real fear behind his worry.

Bella looked up at her husband. The frantic look in his eyes had been replaced by mild concern.

He rubbed his forehead and released a long sigh. "Please let me know next time you leave to go somewhere."

"I will, I promise." Bella placed her hands on top of his wondering where all this worry had come from.

Jack put both hands over hers, his thumb lightly caressing the skin on the back of her hand. His tender touch brought warm tingles to her skin that shot up her arm like thousands of tiny prickles of heat. His hazel eyes burned like a laser beam into hers.

When Jack leaned down slowly as if to kiss her, Bella panicked.

She loved Jack's kisses, but they needed to remember their relationship was a marriage contract. Theirs was a relationship based on convenience, not on true love.

Bella turned her head to the side to look at her computer in an effort to distract him. "Would you take a look at the latest design I created for the Adventure Park?"

His hazel eyes narrowed slightly and raised one

eyebrow raised, making her aware that he knew she was trying to divert his attention away from kissing her.

Jack stepped close to her, his cheek nearly brushing hers as he leaned down to study the design on her computer screen.

"This design is from ideas I've had rolling around in my head for the princess castle." Bella pointed to the four turrets that graced each side of the castle walls.

The interior had the wide stone staircase leading to an upstairs balcony that overlooked the entrance. There were more rooms as you climbed the staircase to the third floor where there was a large room for each of the four corners.

Bella clicked her mouse to open up a larger version of the design and she explained to Jack, "When we visited the Theme Park in Paris, I was inspired by the design and it gave me some new ideas."

She pointed to the layout she had on the computer screen and asked, "What do you think?" Bella turned to look at Jack.

The corners of his mouth turned up into a wide grin. "This is a really great design, Bella. I can tell you've given the details a lot of thought. I'm convinced kids and adults alike will be captivated."

A warmth curled in her belly at his words of praise. "Thanks Jack. There are so many more ideas I have for this Adventure Park." She spoke animatedly. "I had an idea for the Founder's Day Celebration. I would like to put together a 3D model of the designs we have for the *Rose Adventure Park* so the folks of Paradise Lake could get a really good idea of the fun theme park we are creating there. And hopefully when they see the design, they will get excited about it."

"I think it would be great to show folks a model of the Adventure Park design at the Founder's Day celebration, but there's just one drawback." Jack ran one finger down the calendar that hung on her wall.

"What's that?"

"The Founder's Day celebration is in less than two weeks. Do you think that's enough time to put a 3D model together?"

Bella nodded. "I do. A friend from college specializes in visualization products. I think she'll be able to get this done quickly."

"Okay. Let's do it." Jack stood up a big smile on his face.

"Now, we just need more of the townsfolk in Paradise Lake to get excited about this theme Park, because maybe that will sway the town council in our favor."

"Maybe." Jack rubbed his chin thoughtfully before his gaze looked back at her. "You've got some great ideas, Bella."

"Thanks Jack." Bella relished his words of praise. She knew it was rare for Jack to give compliments, so words of appreciation were all the more meaningful coming from him.

Jack nodded and walked to the door before he turned in her direction. "Don't forget my Grandparents, Mom and the rest of the family will be here tomorrow for our monthly get-together."

"I look forward to it, Jack." Bella gave him a big smile as he left her office.

Bella rested her head against the back of her chair and sighed.

As much as she adored Jack's family, she had to admit she was a little on edge about seeing them.

She was grateful Elle would be there, so at least she had someone in the family that understood her.

Yet, Bella worried that her and Jack wouldn't be able to convince the rest of the Stevenson family they were in love.

❧

"What a lovely place to have a picnic." Catherine Stevenson walked beside Bella toward the sandy beach in front of Jack's lake.

"It is beautiful, isn't it?" Bella carried one of the picnic baskets and set it on top of the table that Ben and Chipper had set up.

"Bella, you've outdone yourself. This is perfect." Eliza Stevenson walked on Bella's other side, her gaze sweeping over the grassy knoll that overlooked the sandy beach and lake.

Clasping Bella's hand, Eliza leaned over to whisper in her ear. "I'm so happy Jack has you for his wife. I see a change in my son. He's more contented and happy. You're just what he needs."

Heat crept up her neck and spread to her cheeks. "Thanks, Mom."

It felt weird to call Eliza Stevenson, mom. Bella never had the privilege of having a mom in her life, since her own mother died when she was born.

A warmth surrounded her heart at being close to Jack's mom, a kind and generous lady who had been through so much. Eliza's husband had died when her five sons were just starting their teen years and she had raised them on her own.

Bella had so much respect for Jack's mom and her ability to go through those tough times with grace and strength. She hoped that sometime in the not-too-distant-future Eliza would share more of her story.

Jack's mom saw her as a wife who was in love with her son. Her husband's mom saw her as the woman who made her son happy. Bella only saw herself as the token wife for this year only, until Jack found a real wife he actually loved and wanted to marry.

The fact was, both her and Jack needed his family and her Dad to believe they were in love. They didn't want to cause any hurt to Jack's grandparents, his mom or her Dad. They loved and respected them too much to let a fake marriage be the cause of pain.

Bella caught a glimpse of her Dad walking beside Nurse Marmie leaning on her for support. He looked over at her a happy grin on his face.

At least her Dad was honest about his growing love for Marmie.

She on the other hand, felt like a fraud.

Bella glanced over to see the source of her irritation — her fake husband — walking ahead of them beside his Granddad. They seemed like they were in a deep conversation. Jack glanced over at her, a rogue smile hovering over his lips.

Her husband wore a white t-shirt and jean shorts that

emphasized his long tanned legs and muscular arms. Jack was so good looking and charming that it was difficult to resist his appeal.

She had to continually remind herself that Jack was only pretending to love her. Sometimes the way her husband's hazel eyes zeroed in on hers or the tender touch of his hand, caused her awareness of him to intensify to the point where Bella was convinced she was falling in love.

But she didn't want to let her thoughts go down that rabbit hole. She couldn't let herself be trapped. She couldn't let herself lose control. She couldn't let herself fall in love.

However, neither could she dwell on the fact that Jack had married her to get his great-grandfather's inheritance.

In some ways Bella felt like she didn't have any other choice. It was either marry Jack or they would've drowned in debt from her Dad's medical bills and they would've lost the only home she'd ever known.

She had done what she needed to do. Now, she needed to make the best of it.

Bella led the Stevenson family to the plushly cushioned wicker furniture that they placed on the grass under the shade of the poplar trees. A large coffee table rested between the wicker sofas to rest their drinks. Bella had scoured the area, before she created this pillowy soft oasis so near the sandy beach of the lake.

"Bella, I think I might just stay here forever. This is beautiful." Elle laughed as she sat down and put her feet up.

"Elle, as much as I would like to grant your wish, I'm

afraid we'd still have to get you to the hospital within the month." Adam reached a gentle hand to massage his wife's baby belly.

"I suppose so. And here I was hoping to make this place my new refuge away from the world." Elle giggled.

"You can come here as often as you like, Elle. I love this place too." Bella said softly as she looked out at the lake.

Soon everyone was talking about the soon-to-be arrival of Elle and Adam's baby.

"Have you found out if your baby is a boy or a girl?" Bella relaxed against the cushioned sofa. Jack seated himself next to her, his arm around her shoulders. Bella shivered with a growing awareness of her husband's touch as his fingers drew gentle circles on her shoulders.

"We wanted to keep it a surprise, so we won't know until the baby is born." Elle smiled at her husband. Adam pulled his wife close to his side.

"We're excited to find out." Adam lifted Elle's hand to his lips and kissed it.

Bella saw the loving way Adam treated his wife and sighed. She looked around and saw Jack's Granddad and Grandmom sitting close beside each other holding hands.

These couples held a deep and lasting love for each other that Bella couldn't quite understand, but knew it was something she desperately wanted for herself.

"The buffet table for lunch is ready to enjoy." Ben walked over to announce that it was time to eat.

Mrs. Potter was already waiting for them, busy organizing all the food on the tables that were under the shade of the pop-up beach canopy. Chipper and Ben were by her side helping.

Catherine walked next to Bella as they approached the buffet table. They carried their picnic style food of light sandwiches, salads and other finger food to the sitting area.

"Bella, come sit beside me for lunch. I'd like to get to know you better." Catherine patted the seat beside her. "Looks like both our husbands decided to go off on their own anyway."

"Of course." Bella nodded at Catherine and sat down. She glanced over quickly to see Jack in what seemed to be a deep conversation with his Granddad.

"So tell me what's it like being married to my grandson so far?" Catherine took a delicate sip of her iced tea, her eyes filled with curiosity as she looked at her new granddaughter.

Bella set her plate of food on the coffee table and held a glass of lemon water in her hand as she thought about what to say.

"Well, Jack is like no other." The corners of her lips curled up as she thought of her husband. "He can be pushy in order to get the details exactly as he wants, which I discovered when he bought clothes for me in Paris."

Bella recalled that with many of the dresses she'd tried on, Jack had asked for something similar but in a different color or size. He had wanted to get clothes that were perfect for her.

Bella continued. "Yet, at the same time he can be surprisingly generous and thoughtful. He took me to a rare bookstore in Paris and even bought me a first edition of the book *Pride and Prejudice* by Jane Austen. I'd dreamed of owning a first edition of that novel since I was a teenager." Bella shook her head bewildered and a little confused by her husband.

"Pushy to get what he wants and yet surprisingly generous, yes that sounds exactly like our Jack." Catherine smiled and her gaze wandered over at where Jack stood talking to his Granddad. "The apple doesn't fall far from the tree."

Bella grinned at that. "So you're saying that Jack got his nature from his Granddad?"

"Well partly from his Stevenson forbears, but also from what he's been through in the past."

"What do you mean?" Bella was really curious to learn more about Jack so she could understand him better.

"Well, I'm not sure if you know about Jack's background Bella, but all five of Eliza and Daniel's sons struggled to make ends meet after their father passed away suddenly. Jack was only fourteen at the time." Catherine's eyes misted over a little as she remembered. "They made it through that time and it bonded them closer as a family. All those boys ended up going to College, but they never forgot that their father died suddenly because of the stress caused him when their Dad's partner took all their money."

"So finding ways to help other people became their passion."

"That's right. But it was during college that Jack got a little wild for a time and that's when he met Elin. It seemed like they were married almost as soon as they met. But the most difficult time for Jack was after his wife left him. She was in a car accident that killed both his wife and unborn son. Jack was devastated." Catherine sighed deeply before continuing. "It was too much for Jack. So, he built this massive home here on the hill and has basically been hiding here for the past four years."

"He's gone through so much heartache." Bella wiped a tear that had snuck it's way down her cheek.

Jack's Grandmom smiled gently. "That's true, but all that pain has made him too afraid to love. He's been too afraid of trusting another woman and misreading her motives. He's afraid of being hurt, so he pushes people away before he can be hurt by them." Catherine leaned closer to Bella and whispered. "That's why I'm so glad he has you by his side to show him how to trust again. I'm glad my grandson has you to show him how to love again."

Something in her tone made Bella's heart ache for Jack. In the past few days she had been the one pushing Jack away. She'd been the one who had been terrified by the power of her own emotions.

Maybe it was time for her to let down her walls to open up her heart to the possibility of loving her husband.

She squeezed Jack's Grandmom's hand, sitting with her in silence for a long time digesting her words.

Perhaps, it was time to let go of fear and embrace love.

CHAPTER TEN

Jack

"I FEEL MORE secure about keeping documents at home with this new room you've designed, Jack." Senator John Carver shook his hand. "Now we just need to figure out where those stolen documents went to."

"I really hope you find those papers soon and the person who stole them."

Senator Carver had told Jack privately that the stolen documents were related to suspicious behavior of Senator Ivan Wolffe.

It seemed that Senator Wolffe's actions and words of his campaign didn't seem to match up. Ivan Wolffe was the oldest of the two Wolffe brothers who served on Paradise Lake's town council.

Jack hoped the brothers weren't dishonest in all their dealings, but it was starting to look like his hopes were about to be dashed.

Any lack of integrity by politicians who were there to serve the people troubled Jack.

"Yeah me too. But at least from now on, the documents in this room will be safe from prying eyes." The Senator turned his head to stare at the completed secret room that Jack had just finished. It was hidden behind a large bookshelf that spanned the length of their living room with only the Senator and his wife knowing the access code.

"Glad I could help, John. Have a great weekend." Jack grinned and hurried to his truck and drove home, happy to have helped another person feel safer in their everyday life.

Each security design project he completed for someone, made Jack feel like he was doing something right. The ruin that his father, mom and brothers faced when their father's business partner stole their money spurred Jack on to continue doing what he could to help as many people as possible to feel safer and more secure.

As he drove up the mountain towards home, Jack thought of his new wife. He had barely seen Bella for three days. She'd been so busy finishing the Rose Adventure Park designs and he had been busy completing the Senator's secret room that they were like ships passing in the night.

Parking his truck in front of the house, Jack had an idea that would give both of them a much needed break. He only hoped his wife would agree to it.

He hurried into the house and found Mrs. Potter in the kitchen and told her of his plan.

"Well, I hope you can get your wife to leave her office long enough to eat, Jack. She's as thin as a rail. Too much stress if you ask me." Mrs. Potter shook her head and wiped her hands on her apron.

"I'm going to try to get her to take a break."

"Good luck with that." Mrs. Potter's concern for Bella, made Jack aware of how much he had neglected her the past few days.

Hurrying down the hallway, he reached Bella's office and knocked. He didn't hear anything, so he opened the door only to see Bella glued to her computer screen.

"Bella." Jack walked into the room, but she didn't seem to hear him. He walked behind the desk, put his head beside hers and whispered. "Wake up, Beauty."

Startled, she jumped back in her chair. "Jack, I didn't even hear you knock."

"Well I did knock, but you were concentrating so hard that you didn't hear me." Jack winked at her.

"I guess. I think I only have one more day's work and I'll have this design finished and ready for you to take a look at it. So I should get back to work."

Bella put her hands back on her keyboard. Jack leaned his hips on the edge of the desk beside her, staring at his beautiful wife. With her hair up in a scrunchy and a pencil stuck in middle, she looked like a mixture between street urchin and serious student.

Without warning he grasped her hands, his gaze studying her intently.

Surprised, she looked up at him, her eyes big and

round as pink blossomed in her cheeks. "Jack what are you doing?"

"This afternoon, I don't think you should go back to work."

"What? Why ever not?"

"Because my beautiful workaholic, you need a break. And I have a great idea that involves the two of us going into the great outdoors today."

"Jack, I really can't. I've got to get this done."

Jack leaned closer until his forehead touched hers and whispered. "Your boss insists."

He kissed her forehead and leaned back eyeing her critically. "Mrs. Potter told me you've gotten much too thin and I happen to agree. You need fresh air and lots of food. I think a picnic is in order."

"A picnic?"

Jack laughed as her eyes widened in confusion. He reached for Bella's hand pulling her behind him. "Yes, a picnic. I want to show you the Silver Mine and then I want to take you to see some awe-inspiring scenery of the mountain and down to the lake."

Bella followed him into the hallway and sighed. "Give me ten minutes to change my clothes then." She sighed looking down at her rumpled sweat pants.

"It's a beautiful sunny day. Bring along some shorts and a t-shirt so you can enjoy the sun." Jack called after her as she went to her room to change.

Jack was waiting for her at the large front entrance when she arrived ten minutes later. She wore jean shorts and a blue t-shirt, both pieces of clothing that emphasized her curves. He realized too late, that maybe it would've been wiser for him to suggest she wear baggy jeans and a sweatshirt.

Brahms wagged his tail and slipped his head under Bella's hand just asking to be petted. Bella reached down to hug him and slipped her outdoor running shoes on.

They walked outside into the sunshine and Jack put the picnic basket in the back of the two-seater ATV. Brahms sat in between them as they followed the well-worn trail that led to Grand's mine. Bella held the large picnic basket while Jack drove.

Brahms' tail wagged wildly as they drove through the large patch of trees.

Thirty minutes later they reached a large clearing.

"Oh Jack, it's beautiful here." Bella's stopped suddenly her gaze spreading from the mountains around them to the green valley below.

"I see you've hired workers for the Silver Mine." Bella gaze shifted to the valley where many miners hurried in and out of the mine.

As they drove toward the workers, Jack explained, "Since I've now inherited Grand's mine, I saw no reason to wait. I've always wanted to dig deeper and further back."

When they reached the mine, it was a beehive of activity.

They hopped out of the ATV and Jack told Brahms to stay.

Jack walked over to talk to his foreman who was in charge of the workers.

"Hey Mike. Got a few minutes to show us around?"

Jack spoke to the man who nodded and handed Jack and Bella each a hardhat.

Jack turned to Bella and slipped a hardhat on her head and placed one on himself as well. "We'll follow Mike. It'll be easier as he knows where the workers are and how to navigate the inside of the mine to reach the different areas without getting hurt."

They followed Jack's foreman into the cave.

Loud sounds from the machinery and sometimes the loud conversations from the miners around them made it impossible to hear one another. It wasn't until they had walked further inside, that the noise quieted and they were able to have a conversation.

"This is where it forks off into three separate tunnels." Mike pointed to the dark caverns up ahead." It's easy to get lost, so you have to know which tunnel leads to where. We'll follow this one to the left, because it'll take us to the original site."

Jack felt Bella's hand slip inside his. He squeezed her hand, knowing she didn't like dark enclosed spaces. The light that was attached to their hardhats was what helped them finagle their way through the dark passage.

After a long walk they finally arrived.

"This is the original site location from years ago when Walker Stevenson bought the mine in the early 1920s." Mike pointed to a section of the tunnel just ahead.

"I remember this spot." Jack walked farther ahead and ran one hand along the solid dirt-packed wall. "When I was ten years old, Grand showed me a silver thread that ran down that part of the mine. At the time, Grand told me he didn't have the energy to hire the workers needed, but he said one day I would find the treasure that was here."

Bella followed him studying the solid wall of dirt. "I see a thin line of something grey and also a strain of something yellowish along this side. Does that mean there are minerals here to mine?"

"It means there's a possibility of minerals. As soon as we get the team here, we'll dig deeper to see what we find." As Mike spoke he was also studying the wall opposite them and making marks along the wall. "We'll be starting to mine this area next week, so we'll keep you updated as to what we find."

"How exciting." Bella said as they began the long walk back to the mine's entrance.

Finally they stepped out into the sunlight.

"Thanks Mike for the tour." Jack shook his hand.

"Anytime, Jack. I'll send you the first report at the end of next week." Mike took their hardhats and put them in a nearby bin.

"I look forward to hearing from you." Jack grinned and grabbing Bella's hand they walked together to the ATV. Brahms was there waiting for them wagging his tail at them like they'd been gone a week.

As they climbed into the ATV, Jack turned to Bella and asked. "What did you think of the Silver Mine?"

Brahms jumped up and squatted between them.

Jack scratched behind his ears, Brahms tongue hung out the side of his mouth and he leaned in for more attention.

"Honestly? I found it big, dark and a little scary, but I'm excited to see what the workers discover as they begin mining that area next week." Bella grinned as she slipped one arm around Brahms.

"Me too. We'll see if Grand had the right idea about mining deeper in the original site." Jack started the ATV and drove slowly along the open field.

"Where are we headed now?" Bella's question could barely be heard above the wind blowing in his ears.

"To the lake." Jack winked at her as he began to drive down the old dirt road that led from the mine down the hill to the twenty acres of lakefront property he had bought a few years ago.

Jack stopped the ATV near the lake and turned off the engine. "This is it."

"Oh Jack, it's gorgeous here. Now I see what all the fuss has been about."

Bella's eyes grew wide as her gaze swept the area. There were large poplar trees that ran along the edge of the land and farther back were rolling hills. Trees separated the land from the sandy beach in front of the lake. There was a small cabin and a boat-house on the lakefront.

"Yes it is quite nice. That's why I thought this would be the perfect place for the *Rose Adventure Park*." Jack stepped around to the back of the ATV. Looking around he expelled a long breath.

"It is the perfect place. We just need to convince the town council." Bella realized she hadn't told Jack the latest news yet. "Dad told me this morning that there was a town hall meeting last night about new by-laws they're putting in place. They also had a discussion about new businesses that would affect the town like the Adventure

Park." Bella was still a little tense after hearing the news this morning. "You were out of town on that new project and I was locked in my office trying to finish this design. But Dad and Marmie went to the meeting."

"What did your Dad have to say?" Jack rubbed the back of his neck.

"It seems that many people think your theme park is a good idea. Dad said there were some who made rude comments. One mother asked how a Beast like Jack Stevenson could create a theme park and still expect parents or grandparents of young children to bring them anywhere near him." Bella frowned. "How people can be rude like that, is beyond me."

A grimace formed around her lips. "But, some folks on the town council are undecided. Mayor Rainey is one of them and so is the oldest person on the council, Mrs. Marple. Other members of the council love your idea. Of course you already know that the Wolffe brothers don't like your project and have convinced the newest council member, Mason Rogers that your project is a bad idea too."

"Hmm. Well I can't say I'm surprised. We'll need to somehow get the Mayor and Mrs. Marple to see the benefits of having our own Adventure Park in Paradise Lake." Jack ran a hand through his hair as his gaze studied this twenty acres of land.

"That's why I suggested to Mayor Rainey that you would be the best person to give the speech at the Founder's Day Celebration this year. That way you can talk about why you're so passionate about this adventure park."

"Bella, what were you thinking to tell them I would speak in front of that crowd?" Jack unconsciously touched his scar, something Bella noticed he did when he felt overwhelmed or stressed.

Bella stepped closer to him. "Jack, it'll be okay. It's only for ten minutes. This is your chance to talk about your Great-Grandfather and the passion he had for Paradise Lake and how that passion has carried over to you and your brothers. Folks will see that and be inspired to get on your side."

"Bella, I don't think this is a good idea." Jack looked away for a moment before staring back at her. Bella saw a haunted look in his eyes. "It's been so long since I was really out in public. I mean, I think I've terrified enough people don't you think?"

"Jack, that's not what I see. Looking at you right now, I see a man who is successfully designing much needed safety systems and also fun projects for others. I also see a man who loves his family and is dedicated to creating a place that will bring happiness to many kids."

Bella reached up and gently touched the scar on his right cheek. "It doesn't matter about the scars, Jack. In fact, I think what you've gone through only makes what you have to say even more meaningful."

Jack covered her hand with his. Her cheeks blossomed pink with his attention. His heart softened at Bella's words and dispelled some of his fears. Bella made him feel better than he'd ever felt before.

Her belief in him, made Jack want to be all those wonderful things she thought he was. Her belief in him ignited a spark in him to want to give that talk to the townsfolk to let them see his side. Her belief in him, made him want to let down the self-imposed walls, to let others see him for who he really was.

Bella wasn't like Elin, pretending to love him only to set him up for disappointment. She didn't care about the scar on his face. She only saw what could be, even though he'd been gruff and abrupt with her in the past few weeks.

For a moment, Jack looked down at the soft hand that was enfolded in his and fingers that intertwined with his own. It was difficult to see where her hand ended and his began. *Almost like they were meant to be.*

Bella followed his gaze and gently pulled her hand out of his. Her fingers twirled a long strand of her long brown hair, a sure sign that she was feeling skittish. He noticed little quirks about her in the past few weeks, little signs that let him know when he had gotten too close.

A small smile formed around his mouth dispersing some of the tension.

"We'll convince the town council yet, Jack."

Jack nodded realizing that Bella had read his mind again. A grimace formed on his lips as he reached for the picnic basket. "Are you hungry?"

"Famished."

"Well then, let's go and find a shady spot." Jack walked with Bella beyond the trees to the sandy beach. He spread out the picnic blanket on a small hill that overlooked the blue lake.

Bella opened the basket, pulling out sandwiches, veggies, fruit and many types of pastries and squares.

"It would seem that Mrs. Potter thinks she's feeding an

army instead of just the two of us." Jack chuckled as he settled himself on blanket.

"The three of us. I found food for Brahms in the basket too." Bella put food in one dish and bottled water in another for Jack's dog. Bella laughed as Brahms began eating right away.

Bella sank down onto the blanket.

As they began to eat sandwiches, Jack enjoyed the heat of the sun surprised at how at ease he felt with Bella today. Bella had been happy to go to the silver mine with him in spite of her fear of enclosed spaces. She continued to amaze him by how she willingly gave of herself to others.

Bella had taken Elle with her to the Stevenson Safe-House earlier this week and they had spent the afternoon with Dani, Bree and the other girls there. Not to mention all the hours she had already spent designing the *Rose Adventure Park.*

Looking over at her, he noticed her tired eyes. The dark circles under her eyes were tell-tale signs of too many late nights.

"Didn't sleep much last night?"

Bella looked up at him, her cheeks darkening to red. "Not so much." She reached into the picnic basket and grabbed a couple of bottled waters. She offered him one before taking a long drink, studying him over the rim.

"I saw your office light on when I went to grab a book from the Library late last night." Jack moved closer to her breathing deeply of her flowery scent. Taking this time to sit outside in the fresh air was a perfect way to spend the afternoon. What made it even better, was being close to Bella.

"Yeah, I've been working hard trying to refine the designs for the Adventure Park." Bella waved her arm as if to encircle the whole twenty acres. "I just have a few more tweaks and then I'll show them to you to see if the new changes meet your approval." As she grinned, her brown eyes and pearly white smile sparkled, captivating him.

"I can't wait to see it." He was caught under her enchantment and was sure he would approve almost anything she asked. "Your previous designs were good. I'm interested to see how you could make these better."

"Well, you'll just need to wait until I'm finished."

"Speaking of being finished, did you get a chance to send the images to your friend who does the 3D design modelling?" Jack toyed with the water bottle in his hand as he looked at her.

"Yes. She said we should expect to hear back from her either today or tomorrow."

Jack sighed. "Good because there's only three days left until the Founder's Day celebration. It'll be good to show-case the *Rose Adventure Park* alongside other businesses and events in the area." Jack sat up and looked across the lake to all the homes that were part of Paradise Lake community.

Bella studied Jack, following his gaze to see those folks who were boating on the lake and the homes that surrounded the lake.

She turned to look at him. "You really love this area don't you?"

"I do. Grand inspired a dream of building a better community inside each of us boys as we were growing up. It must've caught on." Jack couldn't help but fondly remember his stalwart great-grandfather. "I think that's one of the reasons why I hired workers to dig deeper into the mine. I don't want to have any regrets that I didn't try my best to try to find the treasure that Grand insisted was there."

"I'm glad you're doing that Jack. It's important to do what we can to try to find the treasure we're looking for - or else we'll always wonder what could've been."

"That sounds like a deep thought."

Bella's cheeks turned pink and she looked away for a moment. "Maybe. But it doesn't make it any less true."

Jack grunted in response.

Bella's voice sounded genuinely distressed. "Do you still feel a loyalty and love for this town in spite of how mean some folks have been to you?"

Jack paused for a second before he turned and shrugged. "Well I really don't like it that the townspeople call me Beast or that mothers hurry the other way with their small children when they see me coming."

Bella's mouth fell open slightly. "You know what they call you?"

His deep laugh was sort of half mocking. "The Beast. Yes I've known about that nickname for a long time." Shaking his head from side to side, he breathed out a tired sigh. "I don't have any control over what people say about me. I understand their terror at seeing the hideous face of the Beast."

Jack's gaze studied the small town of Paradise Lake his shoulders taut like an overstressed string on a violin. Even though the accident had happened four years ago, he still tensed whenever he talked about it.

Bella moved closer to him and put her small white hand on his arm. The skin on his arm tingled at the warmth of her touch. "Jack look at me. Please."

He turned his head slowly, his expression stoic and his eyes hooded.

"Just because you have a scar on one side of your face, does not make you terrifying. You do not look hideous. A scar does not a monster — or Beast — make, no matter what folks in town say." Bella moved her hand to the right side of his face and with gentle fingers touched his scar. "You're still Jack Stevenson, successful businessman, kind-hearted son, generous brother and compassionate supporter of the less fortunate. Nothing will ever change that. Their mean words and actions don't change who you are."

Bella's soft words encircled him like a snug cocoon.

Jack found himself drawn to her warmth. He tried so hard to stay away from her. To resist being tempted by his wife.

He'd forced himself to stay away from her. He was constantly reminding himself that Bella was off limits. She was only his fake wife. What they had wasn't real.

But hearing her words, Jack's heart thawed a little bit more. It seemed his wife had discovered one of the secrets to melt a little more of the block of ice that encircled his heart.

Jack reached his hand to cover hers. He lifted her small hand from his cheek and placed a soft kiss on the inside of her palm.

"How do you know just what I need to hear?" Jack peered over at her.

Bella shrugged. "I don't know. I just sense things and then feel like I need to speak the truth as a way of combating the lies you've heard from others."

"I'm glad I've got you in my corner." Jack stared at his wife, unable to look away.

Her eyes moved away from his and slipped down to focus on his lips. Quickly, she looked down at their clasped hands and tried to move away from him, to slip her hand out of his.

Jack didn't know what came over him, but he couldn't let her move away.

He needed to get closer. He needed to taste her sweet lips. Tugging on the hand he still held, he pulled her against his chest, slipping his arm around her waist.

Brown eyes stared up at him in silent question before Jack lowered his head and touched his lips to hers. His lips closed possessively over hers, searing her name on his heart.

He pulled her onto his lap, needing her close.

"Jack..." Bella started to protest, but that lasted for only a moment before her body melted in his embrace. Jack wrapped his arms protectively around her, kissing her with a fiery tenderness, fitting and shaping her lips against his own.

He explored the soft recesses of her mouth until she trembled.

Consuming kisses followed and Jack felt like he was on fire. Sensations that Bella awakened in him had been dormant far too long. He was afraid his heart was awakening to love and worried that he didn't know how to put a stop to it.

Without warning, a loud splash shot through the silence followed by a series of booming barks.

Bella broke away from Jack's kisses to see Brahms running through the edge of the lake chasing a much smaller dog. Close on his heels was a young boy running along the water's edge.

"I think someone is trying to catch his dog." Bella pushed lightly against Jack's chest and stood to her feet, her legs shaky from their shared kisses.

Jack pushed to his feet and swooped down to give her one more kiss. "I'll be back. I promise, we'll finish this later."

As he chased after his dog, all Jack could think of were his wife's sweet kisses.

His fake wife was proving to be more passionate and captivating than he originally expected.

All of a sudden, his heart was tumbling over and over with a new yearning for more of Bella's affections. He didn't know how to stop these new desires from growing.

Did he even want to?

ella

"LET me carry that for you, Bella. You already have your hands full." Jack took the newly finished 3D design of the *Rose Adventure Park* and they walked the short distance to the Paradise Lake Community Center.

"Thanks Jack." Bella looked up at her husband, heat rising to her cheeks as she remembered his kisses from the other day. He had awakened in her a new awareness of the possibilities for their marriage. Even now, her heart wondered was love possible for them?

She peered up at him only to find Jack's hazel eyes darkening as his gaze swept over her face. Warmth rose up her neck, coloring her cheeks.

The stubble on his face had grown to the point where today his beard covered much of the scar. Bella was sure he did that on purpose, knowing he would be speaking today.

Yet, with his beard he looked even more like a pirate and she liked it.

Bella adjusted the laptop case that hung from her shoulder, uncomfortable with where her thoughts were going.

As they entered the community center she saw many of the townsfolk setting up their tables. Loud voices all around them, made it difficult for them to communicate as they searched for their booth.

The town had let non-profits and businesses know that whoever wanted to participate, could have a table at today's event. It was great to be a part of the community.

For this Founder's Day celebration, the mayor and a few others were scheduled to speak later. She was happy Jack had agreed to speak even though she could tell he was nervous.

Bella looked around at the ever-growing crowd. "Looks like a lot of people showed up." She wiped the tables that they'd been given and began to set up her computer. She located the website she'd designed for the *Rose Adventure Park* and searched for the video she'd made.

Jack set the 3D Model of the adventure park on the table. It was quite large and took up half of the table's space. "I wanted to tell you Bella, you really did an amazing job with the website and with the 3D model of the Adventure Park. You even added little details like the moat around the Princess Castle and the blue water falls for the water ride."

Jack traced a finger over each design element before peering up at her.

"I'm thrilled you like it. I just hope that there will be something here that will attract more parents and children to your Adventure Park." Bella sighed as she finished setting up.

"You've put so much time and effort into this project. Since we're working together as a team, I see it more as ours."

"I appreciate that, Jack." A whisper of warmth trailed from her stomach to her throat and she swallowed back a surge of emotion at his words. She loved it that he thought of them as a team.

Bella continued to keep busy too afraid she'd turn into a big puddle of tears where she stood. There had been many times in her life when she'd felt alone and discouraged by overwhelm, so to hear Jack say they were in this together meant a lot.

She setup the other table with information for the Stevenson BeSafe non-profit which focused on helping victims of human trafficking. She double-checked that the slideshow of the two safe houses in Seattle as well as pictures of Elle and the horse therapy program were working. As she finished the setup, Ben, Mrs. Potter and Chipper arrived.

Folks from town began walking through the large building, first trickling in and before long there was a large crowd.

Children were really excited to see the colorful 3D model of the adventure park, with the Princess castle, the

Pirate ship and the many rides that were sculpted into the design.

"I like the Mama Squirrel and Ribble the Rabbit in this video mom." A cute little girl tugged on her mother's hand and led her to the video.

"Are you building a theme park outside of Paradise Lake?" The mom asked Bella.

"We hope to. We need more folks to convince the town council that this theme park is a good idea, then this project should be given the green light so we can start building." Bella handed her a brochure with more details. "If you're curious, take a look through this and go to our website for updates on this project."

"I will. It would be exciting to have an adventure park nearby. You have my vote." The woman and her little girl walked away and Bella grinned at Jack.

"It's a start. We need a lot more interest to get this off the ground."

Over the next few hours, more people stopped by, some showing a lot of interest in their plans for the Adventure Park and some not so much.

A well-dressed woman who looked to be in her mid-twenties approached their table, a furrow deepening between her brows. "You're planning a theme park near this quiet town? For some of us, the reason we moved to Paradise Lake is to enjoy the peaceful idyllic setting of a small town. If this terrible idea goes through, our town will become as busy and noisy as a big city."

She waved one hand over the 3D model of the Adventure Park design and spoke again. "I certainly don't support this idea."

"Sorry to hear that, ma'am." Jack stepped forward to talk to the obviously frustrated lady. "If you take a look at our website, you'd see a step-by-step proposal on how we plan to minimize the amount of noise the park makes when in operation. Our goal is to create a family friendly atmosphere with as little noise as possible."

The woman crossed her arms over her chest. "Well, I really can't see that happening." She looked at Jack, creases on her forehead deepening as she went on, "And I can certainly understand why a man like you, with your marred appearance, wouldn't be able to appreciate the importance of appearance and feel for a theme park here in Paradise Lake. I hope this little project of yours never gets off the ground. If it does, it'll ruin this town. I would rather see condos or hotels built along the lake than this eye-sore." Huffing she walked away from their table.

Bella watched as Jack stood there for a moment, his lips in a thin line and his jaw clenched. She could tell by looking at him, that he was angry. She realized people judged Jack unfairly about what he could or couldn't do based on his marred appearance. It wasn't right.

A new awareness dawned on her of how difficult it must be for her husband to live with people's rude comments everyday. A wave of compassion sparked inside of her.

Jack slowly expelled a breath.

She stepped beside him and slipped her hand in his, squeezing gently.

Jack's gaze focused on Bella, seeing in her eyes acceptance for who he was. He didn't know how long he stood there before they were interrupted.

"Chipper, there you are. Slow down dear boy, before you run someone over." Mrs. Potter got her grandson's attention just in time before he ran into a toddler.

Mrs. Potter shook her head as Chipper ran up to them. "I think we've given away over three hundred brochures already." Chipper came back with Ben by his side. "We need a whole lot more."

"Wow, that's great. Thanks for your help Chipper. I'm glad you're so eager for folks to hear about this new theme park." Bella gave him another large bundle of brochures.

"Of course I am, Mrs. Stevenson. I ain't — er, I mean haven't — ever been on theme park rides before. I'm really looking forward to going with Grandma." Chipper's ten-year old voice was full of excitement.

Mrs. Potter at one time had told Bella that Jack had paid for private tutors for Chipper so when he graduated High School he'd be accepted into some of the best Universities. Now it seemed like Chipper's tutors were helping him with his grammar too.

Jack continued to surprise her with the thoughtful things he did for those he cared about.

Mrs. Potter reached an arm around her grandson and whispered. "I'm looking forward to going on rides with you too, love. Now, see if you can give those all away." She kissed the top of his head and let him go.

Without warning the announcer's voice came over the speakers interrupting them. "In a few minutes, Mayor Rainey, Senator Ivan Wolffe, Senator John Carver and Jack Stevenson will share their thoughts on what makes Paradise Lake a great place to live. Just follow the crowd outside. Afterwards, there will be a potluck available for folks who want to stick around."

"Hmm, looks like it's time to bring the food out." Bella began to pack up their things. "And it's time for you to get ready to speak Jack."

"I know. I'm going." Jack saw that Bella was busy trying to get their things organized. "Why don't you go on with Mrs. Potter and Ben will stay here for a little longer just in case there are some latecomers. I'm sure he'll see to it that Chipper is taken care of." Jack put his hand on top of hers.

Tingles of warmth shot up her arm at the touch of Jack's hand on hers. He winked and threw her a guarded-smile and Bella took her cue to get going.

With one last glance at Jack, Bella hurried behind Mrs. Potter. They both carried casserole dishes and large trays of all sorts of sliced of veggies and fruit.

As she stepped outside, warm fresh air hit her along with the scent of barbecued meat and other cooked foods. Noticing the large crowd gathered in front of the stage, she put her hand on her forehead to shadow her face from the bright sun so she could get a better view of who would be speaking today.

Mayor Rainey was there along with Senator John Carver. The other men on stage looked like the Wolffe brothers from the town council. Jack had mentioned Senator Ivan Wolffe would be speaking today.

Before she turned the corner she saw Jack step onto the stage shaking hands with Mayor Rainey.

She really wanted to be part of the audience to soak in every word. But, she would need to do what she could to listen to the speakers while she helped Mrs. Potter prep the food for the potluck. Everything was supposed to be ready to go by six o'clock so they had a little less than an hour.

Bella followed Mrs. Potter toward the makeshift kitchen, when she caught sight of her Dad and Nurse Marmie standing in the crowd talking to some old friends.

"Mrs. Potter, I'll be there in a minute. I just want to talk to my Dad."

"That's fine dear. I know you'll join us soon." Mrs. Potter patted her arm and walked over to where others were preparing food.

Bella walked over to where her Dad was talking within a small circle of his old friends. "Ah, here's my daughter Bella. She is now Jack Stevenson's wife and has taken over the details of designing the Adventure Park."

She shook hands with Dobi Rudgers, who had been friends with her Dad for years. "I was telling your Dad how impressed I was by that 3D Model of the Adventure Park. You have a rare gift for design Bella."

"Thank you Mrs. Rudgers. I do find it exciting to create something beautiful."

"Of course you do. I could hardly believe my ears when your Dad told me you married. I mean you are such a beautiful young woman that I knew you would get snatched up and married in a heartbeat. But imagine my surprise to learn you married Jack Stevenson." The older lady looked over at Jack. "Him, with his pirate-y looks with that scar and you the beauty. I hope he's kind to you, dear." She peered closer into Bella's eyes as if ferreting out the truth.

"Jack is very kind to me." Bella hesitated for a moment, trying to find the right words. "I find most folks here in town have the wrong idea about Jack. Some even call him a beast, which couldn't be further from the truth. Sure, his face is flawed but aren't we all imperfect in one area or another?"

"Too true, my dear. You've the right of it. Shouldn't have listened to the rumors of course." The older lady patted Bella on the shoulder. "You tell Jack we are excited for the opening day of his Adventure Park. We'll be there with our grandchildren."

Bella grinned. "I'll be sure to tell Jack. He'll be pleased."

Her Dad's friends had wandered away, leaving Dad and Marmie alone so she could talk to them.

"I'm glad you're here, Dad and Marmie. It's nice to have some family on our side when it feels like there are many who aren't." Bella hugged them both.

Her Dad gave her a big smile. "Where else would we be lassie?"

"You really did a fine job with that design, Bella." Marmie's gentle smile and kind words, reminded Bella once again why her Dad had fallen in love with her.

"Well, I just wanted to tell you I appreciate the fact that you both are here today."

"Ah Beauty. There's no other place I'd rather be." Her Dad reached for her and pulled her into one of his massive bear hugs. "And just so you know, your design is better than my original one. You've done well, lassie."

Bella swallowed back tears. "Thanks Dad. I needed to hear that today."

She turned to see the Mayor walk up to the microphone, and saw the people sitting down. "I need to go find Mrs. Potter. I'll see you both a little later."

Hurrying to the kitchen, she found Mrs. Potter bustling about trying to find the right toppings to add to each casserole.

"Bella, if you would cut up those fruit and veggies, that would be great. There's a lot of them so it would be helpful to have you working on it." Mrs. Potter gave her a small knife to get started.

"Sure thing, Mrs. Potter." Bella smiled turned to where the large trays were laid out.

Soon she was busy chopping vegetables into thin slices so folks could enjoy some healthy finger-food snacks. As she worked, Bella overheard snippets of what the speakers were saying.

Mayor Rainey's high-pitched voice weaved in and out over the microphone. "… And we're happy for the many ways the good folks of Paradise Lake have made this town a better place through the years. We're grateful for each of the businesses for their donations to put on this festival and for all the businesses and non-profits who came out today to share what they are doing to make this town and state a better place to live."

The Mayor paused before going on, "But we don't want to stay where we are, we want to keep improving as a town. That's why today, we're happy to have Senator Ivan Wolffe and Senator John Carver speak today. Also Jack Stevenson will be sharing with us today the passion his great-grandfather had for this small town of Paradise Lake when he founded it all those years ago."

Bella finished cutting the veggies and moved onto the

fruit as the microphone crackled and one of the Senators began speaking.

"Many of you know my two brothers Bert and Bart Wolffe who serve on the Town Council of Paradise Lake. Much like my brothers, I have an interest in making small towns like yours, exciting for visitors and profitable for folks who call this home. It's been great to see so many businesses and non-profit who are serving the people in this community. Those that create income for this small town or non-profits are needed."

Senator Wolffe went on, "However, I want to caution the good folks of Paradise Lake to be wary of new start-ups that tell you they are bringing adventure and fun to parents and children when all they're really doing is creating extra noise and an overload of tourists."

A spark of anger ignited inside Bella at Senator Wolffe's words, that he would try to warn the townsfolk against Jack's Adventure Park.

At that moment Chipper walked into the kitchen, interrupting her thoughts.

"Hey Grandma. Can I have some..." Chipper reached for the big pitcher of juice and accidentally tripped and spilled it on the floor.

Bella reached over for some towels to clean it up. She did what she could, but saw they needed to get the mop.

"Chipper why don't you come with me and we'll see if we can find a mop to clean this up, okay?" Bella winked at Mrs. Potter and they walked into the community center and down the hallway to the supply room.

"Here we are. Let's go inside and see what we can find."

Bella opened the door and turned on the light. Chipper followed her inside and they both looked around.

"I found a mop and bucket, Mrs. Stevenson." Chipper picked up the mop. Bella grabbed the bucket and walked to the door. She wanted to get back so she wouldn't miss hearing Jack's speech.

Bella had started to turn the handle to open the door, when she heard voices coming from the other side. She slowly released the door-knob, listening to the conversation in the hallway.

"Are you sure you weren't followed?" A male voice, that held a nasal quality to it, questioned the other person.

"No of course I wasn't followed. I know how to stay away from the careful scrutiny of others." This voice was also male but held a jarring tone. And for some reason to Bella this voice seemed to remind her of someone but she couldn't put her finger on it.

"Mrs. Stevenson…" Chipper was about to go on when Bella turned to him and with one finger to her lips she leaned down to whisper in his ear.

"Let's whisper all right? There are some men outside and I think it's better if we wait until they're done talking before we go, okay?" Chipper nodded, sighing as he sat on the floor.

Bella walked to the door again. She knew she probably shouldn't eavesdrop, but their secretive conversation had her worried. She leaned her ear against the door once more.

"…so that's why we need to make sure folks in this town see the development of the Adventure Park as a bad thing that will really hurt the community." The nasal voice spoke again sure of himself. "I realize you're new to dealing with the goings on in this town, but you have to know how important it is that we do everything we can to stop Jack from getting his Adventure Park up and running."

Bella swallowed quickly, hearing an odd noise coming from her own throat. They were deliberately trying to stop Jack from getting his theme park approved by the town council.

Her hands balled into fists at her side. Her thoughts raced with this new information.

"I know. And I believe I've proven myself capable of getting the job done." The man with the overconfident voice spoke again.

"Yes, you did. That's why we're letting you in on this new idea. Our plan is to build condos and apartments along the strip of beach that borders the town. This will be something that will be quieter than Jack's theme park idea, but will bring in even more money."

"I agree. I think Jack Stevenson needs to be taken down a peg or two. He owns too much property and has too much influence around here. But, I want to know what's in it for me?"

"We'll give you a cut of the profits from selling the condos, making you rich." The nasal voice coughed and a hand slapped the other man on the shoulder.

"I'm in. What do you need me to do?"

Right at that moment, Chipper dropped his mop on the hard floor. Bella froze and walked over to Chipper. "Only a few more minutes okay?" She gave him a quick hug and motioned him to try to be silent.

By the time she walked over to the door, she only heard the tail-end of their conversation.

"...And that's all you need to do. Will you do it?"

As the man questioned his cohort, Bella realized she missed hearing what their plans were.

"Yes, I will. But for all our sakes, I really hope nobody starts digging deeper, or they'll find out about the money trail."

"Shh... the less said the better. If the Senator ever found out we're blabbing about his plans, we'd be in deep trouble."

"All right." The voices and footsteps walked away and soon were only heard in the distance.

Bella breathed a sigh of relief.

"Chipper, it's time to go back to the kitchen and get that juice mopped up." Bella opened the door and looked both ways before they walked into the hallway.

As she walked back to the kitchen, her stomach clenched into a tight fist. Bella didn't know when she would get a chance to talk to Jack, but realized she couldn't wait.

As soon as possible they would need to figure out what to do about this new threat to their plans for the *Rose Adventure Park*.

She caught the tail-end of Senator Carver's speech as they returned.

"The natural beauty of Paradise Lake is unparalleled. In my mind, so are the good people who call this town their home. As a town, you show generosity and kindness, because year after year you welcome others here to enjoy what you love about your town. I say why not do more of that by embracing the Adventure Park as an addition to the beauty of this place." He paused and looked out at the crowd.

"I find that I disagree with Senator Wolffe's caution about the extra noise, tourists and overall disruption to Paradise Lake. I believe you'll find this town unchanged except you'll have more parents and grandparents who want to meet you and who will want to buy from your stores. Which means more jobs and more economic stability. I believe the *Rose Adventure Park* will only add to the beauty of this place for years to come."

Senator Carver looked behind him. "Thank you for the kind invitation to share some thoughts today, Mayor Rainey. I am happy to have joined you all to celebrate this year's Founder's Day celebration."

The crowd clapped as the Senator sat down.

"Next, we'll hear from Jack Stevenson, great-grandson of Paradise Lake's founding father Walker Stevenson." Mayor Rainey spoke and handed the microphone to Jack.

Bella stood motionless as she watched Jack stand on stage silent for a moment. She looked around and saw his Grandparents, mom, his four brothers and Elle all seated near the stage, big smiles on their faces with their eyes glued to him.

"As you know, I'm not usually one for standing up in front of a crowd. But my beautiful wife insisted." Jack grinned and nodded her way. She smiled back and leaned against the doorpost of the kitchen. "At first I froze at the thought of talking to you today, but then as I thought about my great-grandfather, I remembered his words and his passion for this small town."

Jack took a breath and continued, "Most of you know that Walker Stevenson originally came from Wales to America by ship in the early 1900s. He came with only five dollars in his pocket, but he caught a dream in his heart and made up his mind to pursue it. He started off simply by hauling products between businesses in Seattle. Before long he was able to buy himself a team of horses and a wagon and began freighting between cities and his business continued to grow."

Bella could tell by the small smile on Jack's face that he loved telling this story. "Grand loved the bustle of the city and was grateful for the business he'd generated from it, but when he met and married his wife Hannah — my great-grandmother — they both wanted to live some-where quiet. They drove their wagon out of Seattle until they drove over the hill. Grand told me, seeing how the orange-red hues of the sky hit the water, reminded him of what he imagined Paradise would look like."

Jack paused before continuing, "He decided this was where he wanted to live. He bought the land, over a thou-sand acres and encouraged folks who wanted a more peaceful place to live, to join him and his wife. Within a year, they had twenty-four families who had moved to Paradise Lake. Quite an accomplishment back in those days."

The crowd laughed. "Grand would remind us boys that his dream for this community was that we would find ways to help each other when we were in need, but also to search for ways to bring fun and adventure to the people in this community."

Jack looked out at the crowd and many were listening

closely to his story. "Grand's passion for this place and the people in it is why Adam restored the Horse Racing Park that adjoins Grand's old homestead. And it's why I have a dream to build the *Rose Adventure Park*. People have asked me why I think it would be a good idea to build a theme park outside our small town? It's simple. Our children need more happiness in their lives. None of us know how long we have on this earth and sometimes there are so many difficult times that families and children go through suddenly, that throws their life in turmoil."

Jack gripped the podium and released an unsteady breath into the microphone. Bella could tell he struggled to steady his emotions. "That's what my mom and four brothers experienced when my father passed away suddenly years ago. My dad's business partner cheated him out of all the money in their account and suddenly we were paupers overnight. Dad died because of heart failure related to the stress."

Her husband wiped at his cheek. Bella wiped away her own tears thinking how hard this must be for Jack to share his story in public. "I was fourteen and suddenly our family was wondering how we were going pay our bills and how to find enough money for food. My mom worked full-time but it wasn't enough, so my older brother Adam and I went to work full-time and did our schoolwork in the evenings. My younger three brothers each worked part-time as they got old enough."

"We managed to get by, but for our family it was a sudden and scary overnight change. After that day, we realized the fun and carefree days of childhood were over.

We entered adulthood at a young age and it was really difficult for all of us."

Jack paused for a moment before he spoke again. "But good can come out of hard times. Because of what my family experienced came a new passion. The spark of an idea came to me one day that children and families need to have some place they can find happiness and gain new perspective again from the troubles of their everyday lives. That's how the idea for the *Rose Adventure Park* was born. The name is inspired by my great-grandmother's middle name, Rose."

Looking over at the crowd Jack's smile grew broader. "I hope you've been inspired today by the possibilities we have ahead of us to make Paradise Lake a better place that will bring happiness to even more people. We can do this if we'll just have the courage to grab onto it, together."

As Jack stepped away from the microphone the crowd clapped their appreciation.

Bella didn't hear Mayor Rainey's closing remarks. She stared at Jack a huge smile on her face. Her husband had faced his fear and bravely shared a piece of his heart with this town.

It took courage and a humble heart to share a very personal piece of himself with the people from this small town, some of whom had rejected him.

Her heart skipped a beat and seemed to rise physically in her chest. She was proud of Jack and proud he was her husband.

Breathing deeply, a new awareness niggled its way into her heart.

Bella realized she had done the very thing she wasn't supposed to do.

She had fallen in love with her husband.

Now she had to do whatever it took to show him her love, so they could live a happy life together.

CHAPTER TWELVE

Jack

As soon as Jack stepped down from the stage, he was surrounded by many townsfolk eager to talk with him.

Surprise flooded him at the unexpected emotional toll that speaking to his hometown had on him. He could tell by people's expressions that they were a little stunned to hear their local recluse sharing his story.

Jack couldn't blame them for he had surprised himself.

He really didn't want to do it, but when Bella said it might be his only real chance for people in Paradise Lake to hear his story and the reason behind his passion for creating the Adventure Park, it had pushed him. He didn't want to live with regret of not having tried everything he could to get approval for the Adventure Park.

An older woman with grey hair wearing a purple and black pantsuit approached him. "Why, you're not a beast at all Jack Stevenson." Her brassy comment bewildered him for a second, before he realized who she was. This was Mrs. Marple, a widow and the oldest person on the Town Council.

"I'm happy to hear you say that Mrs. Marple." Jack's gaze focused on the short woman who made up for what she lacked in height, by sheer grit. Even though he didn't always like what she had to say, Jack appreciated the fact that she spoke her mind.

"I liked what you had to say today, young man. Today you've shown respect for your Grandparents and for this community. Respect is something that is sorely lacking nowadays." She paused for a moment, squinting as she eyed him. "You know I never should have listened to the gossip I heard about you from some of the other folks about town. They nearly convinced me you were a bad egg."

She pointed her finger at him and grinned. "But I do believe you'll do us some good young man. I'm going to change my vote on the town council in favor of your Adventure Park. I believe it would be good for all of us."

"I sure do appreciate your belief in me and this project, Mrs. Marple." Jack couldn't help but feel good at the sudden change in his favor. She patted him on the shoulder and soon was talking with someone else.

Jack turned to walk away, but was encircled by his grandparents, mom, Adam and Elle and his three brothers.

"Hey Jack. You did a really good job." Gabe, Luke and Zach all clapped him on the shoulder.

Adam and Elle walked up to him, Elle looking like she could give birth any day now. "Jack it was so great to see you up there. I had to get tissues out. I loved hearing you tell Grand's story." Elle's hand held tightly to her husband's arm and her other hand rested on her protruding belly.

"Ah, thanks Elle. To be honest, I was shaking in my boots. I don't think I want to go through that again." Jack gave her a crooked smile.

"Well, I think you should speak more often." Elle looked at her husband.

"You do have a way with words, Jack." Adam squeezed his arm. "It's something to think about."

His Grandparents walked his way. "Jack, your Great-Grandfather would've been proud today. You did well." Granddad touched his shoulder and looked him in the eye a smile on his face. Grandmom nodded her agreement.

"Jack, I'm sure your Dad was looking down with a big smile on his face." His mom held a tissue in one hand and dabbed a tear from her cheek. Her red-rimmed eyes told him she had shed more than one tear.

"Thanks Mom. I hope so. It means a lot to have you here." Jack pulled his mom into a gentle embrace before he stepped back.

"Of course, Jack. Where else would I be? When Bella told me earlier this week that you'd be speaking today, I rearranged my schedule to be here." His mom winked at him.

Jack was amazed at the support of his family. Warmth

flooded him from the love he was shown by his family. He was overwhelmed by their encouragement. They had been his rock solid foundation that helped keep him from falling after Elin and his unborn son died. Now they were standing by him again, supporting him and encouraging him to step beyond his fears.

"You are all amazing. Thanks for believing in me." Jack swallowed a lump of emotion that threatened to spill over.

"We love you Jack." His mom squeezed his hand. Just then, he looked up to see Bella walking toward him.

"Well, I'm going to chat with some friends. We'll talk a little later okay?" Eliza hugged both Jack and Bella and wandered away. The rest of his family also went in separate directions to talk to friends.

Bella kissed his cheek and hugged him before stepping away. "You did good."

Jack pulled his wife to his side, his arm around her waist. He needed her close to him. He needed her acceptance of him. He needed her unwavering belief in him.

Bella looked up at him a new sparkle glimmering in her large brown eyes. He breathed in deeply of her as his gaze roamed her face. Her beauty continued to catch him by surprise, compelling him to take her somewhere private and thoroughly kiss her.

But he would behave himself, for now anyway.

"So you told my Mom I was going to speak at the Founder's Day celebration?" Jack bent down to whisper in her ear. "I wonder how you could've known I'd be up there sharing, even before I agreed to do it?"

"I was confident you'd see how important it was." A

deep rose color blossomed in her cheeks and she peered up at him a sheepish grin on her face.

Jack's gaze slid over hers and he shook his head and chuckled. "You are a mixture of unpredictability and boldness, my beauty. I don't really understand it, but the unexpected mixture makes you even more captivating."

"I'm glad." Bella's warm breath tickled his ear.

All he really wanted to do was take Bella home and kiss her senseless. But he had to focus on what he needed to do today.

"I see the Senator is finally alone. I'm going to speak to him." He kissed Bella on the cheek.

"When you're finished, I need to talk to you." He saw a hint of fear in her eyes that he must have missed before. "You're worried about something. What is it?"

"It'll keep. First you talk to the Senator. We'll talk later." Bella squeezed his hand and smiled up at him.

"All right. It shouldn't take too long."

As Bella walked back the other way toward his family, Jack mulled over in his mind what could've made her worried today. He would talk to her as soon as he talked with the Senator.

Approaching John Carver, he shook his hand. "Great speech. Thanks for your support of the Adventure Park."

"Of course. I love what you're creating here. However, I must warn you, there are those in your town council who do not like what you're doing." The Senator searched the crowd for a moment before looking back at Jack. "The Wolffe brothers were quite insulting when they spoke of your project. I believe they will try to undermine your attempt to get approval from the town council."

"I'm not surprised." Jack expelled a breath, silent for a moment. "Well, we'll just have to find a way to get approval anyway."

"I have every confidence that you will, Jack. Your heartfelt speech today, went a long way towards bringing more people from Paradise Lake on your side. You are a great man, a great designer and a great leader in this community. People are finally seeing that." John's confidence in him felt like a father's affirmation. Waves of pleasure rolled over Jack at his friend's words.

"I don't know what to say except thank you John. That means a lot coming from you." Jack voice cracked with emotion.

No one else -- outside his own family -- affirmed who he was. It meant so much to hear it from a man whom he respected a great deal.

"I meant every word, Jack." John shook his hand a warm smile on his face. Their conversation was interrupted when someone asked the Senator a question.

Jack looked over the crowd, intent on finding Bella. Spotting her over by the tables talking to Chipper, he walked toward her.

As he walked past the Wolffe brothers standing off to one side, Bart Wolffe stared at Jack a look of unrestrained hostility in his face.

Jack just shook his head. He never did understand the Wolffe brothers and why they were consistently trying to thwart his plans. Why was he the focus of all their animosity? Well, he didn't know what he could do about that so he would just continue to press on.

Soon he reached Bella, Chipper and Ben who were

already seated at a table. Jack grabbed some food and sat at the empty place beside Bella, touching her thigh with his. "It looks like you got everything organized. Where's Mrs. Potter?"

Bella nodded at the canopy cover that was over the kitchen. "Mrs. Potter has found some old friends and has been enjoying herself."

Jack turned to Bella, and noticed she was picking at her food. He leaned into her lightly brushing his shoulder against hers. "You're deep in thought. What's up?" Jack was so close to his wife he could see the light scattering of freckles across her nose.

Bella looked at him, misery etched across her face.

"What is it Bella? I hope you know you can tell me anything. Did someone say something to you?" Jack reached over and wrapped her hand in his.

"I didn't want to say anything yet. I didn't want to ruin your evening." Bella bit her lip, her forehead puckered in misery.

"Now you're only making me more worried. Bella, talk to me. Whatever it is we'll figure it out together." Jack whispered. Seeing the worry in her eyes, he asked, "Should we go somewhere, where there are fewer eyes and ears?"

"Yeah, that's a good idea."

Jack got out of his chair and held out his hand. Bella slipped her hand in his and led her to a quieter spot on the other side of the Community Center building.

"All right, no one's around. Tell me what's wrong." Jack put his hands on his wife's shoulders, his gaze searching hers.

"As I was preparing lunch, there was a spill so Chipper and I had to run to the room where they keep the cleaning supplies. While we were in the supply room, we overheard two men talking in the hallway." Bella explained what she remembered of their conversation. "It sounded like they were going to.do something to 'take you down a peg or two.'"

Jack rubbed the back of his neck as he stood for a minute thinking. "One of them said the Senator would be upset if he knew they'd shared his plans?"

"Yes. So obviously they're working together with one of the Senators?"

"That's what it sounded like." Bella shook her head. "But I don't understand. I thought you and Senator John Carver were friends? Why would he make plans that would cause problems for the Adventure Park?"

"I'm confident they aren't talking about John."

"I realize he's your friend Jack, but not everyone is as they seem on the outside."

"No it's not John, trust me. I just spoke to him. He the one that warned me that the Wolffe brothers are doing whatever they can to hinder our plans with the Adventure Park."

Jack looked up at the sky deep in thought. "Hmm, seems like we stirred up a real hornets nest with this project."

"I'd say." Bella breathed out an unsteady breath. "So how do we stop them from trying to hinder the project from moving forward?"

"Well, I'm not sure. So far it's just empty threats. They

haven't done anything yet, but I'll hire guards for the mine and the adventure park just in case."

"That's a good idea. I'm real worried, Jack." Bella rubbed her arms, her eyes laced with fear.

Jack put his arms around her. "It'll be okay. I'll do whatever it takes to protect you, our family and all the workers at the mine." He kissed the top of her head holding her close.

He didn't know what he'd do if anything happened to Bella. She had become too important to him. Lately, he couldn't even do anything without thinking of how his actions or words would affect his wife. Living in the same house with Bella, was starting to feel a whole lot more than a marriage-in-name-only for Jack.

Jack didn't know how to deal with these new feelings, especially since he'd been down this road before. His first wife had really hurt him when she rejected him. The pain of the past was beginning to cause problems with his relationships in the present and he didn't know how to handle that.

The one thing Jack was sure of was that he couldn't lose Bella. He needed to protect her from whatever the Wolffe brothers or their accomplices had planned.

He stepped back a little and with one hand lifted her chin. Looking into her big brown eyes, he saw a deep fear and worry that he desperately wanted to erase.

Leaning down he touched her sweet lips, a possessiveness taking over. His lips lingered before settling deeper laying claim to his wife.

Their mouths moved together slowly, catching each other's rhythm. When he hesitantly moved his mouth deeper into hers to get a better taste of her, he heard a delicate sigh. His first thought was that he didn't want to stop kissing her, but realized he must. As good as it felt to kiss Bella, Jack didn't want things to get out of hand.

Somehow Jack found the strength to pull away from her. He leaned his forehead against hers as he tried to slow down his racing heart.

"I'm sorry. I got carried away. You're so irresistible, I could kiss you all day." Jack stepped back a little ways and grinned at the pink color that blossomed in her cheeks.

"I ahh… " Bella didn't finish her sentence, flustered by his attention.

Jack leaned his forehead against hers, his breathing rapid. "We should get back. I still need at least one dance with you."

"I'd like that." Her brown eyes sparkled and she tucked her arm in his. They walked back to where the band was playing.

The first song was a faster tune. They moved together in an easy rhythm, Jack swinging her in and out at arms length. All too soon the song ended and his brother Luke was there to dance with Bella.

Jack began dancing with Eliza and his Grandmother while Bella danced with his brothers. Jack continued dancing with Bella's friends Rory and Molly.

He was in the middle of dancing with his mom, when he noticed that somehow Mason had angled his way to Bella's side and was dancing with her.

Jack saw red. Alarm bells went off in his head.

This was Mason who held his wife in his arms. He was

the same guy whom he'd had to pull off Bella a few weeks ago for manhandling her.

Suddenly Jack excused himself, hurrying in their direction.

❧

BELLA HAD BEEN ENJOYING a dance with Jack's brother Zach, when Mason tapped him on the shoulder.

"I believe it's my turn." Zach reluctantly stepped aside to let Mason dance with his sister-in-law.

Bella stiffened in his arms as soon as Mason started dancing with her. "What are you doing?" Bella whispered, anger lacing her words.

"Dancing with you. I wanted to talk to you and I can't do that with Jack hovering over you all the time."

"He is my husband, you know. Married people hover over each other. I hear it's quite normal." Bella frowned and shook her head.

"Well, I still think you got married too fast. Which means you probably did it because you were interested in his money."

Bella expelled an angry breath trying to calm down before she spoke. "How dare you…"

"Hey, I'm not blaming you." Mason continued to dance as if there was nothing wrong and he hadn't just insulted her.

"But I'm here to tell you, if it's a rich guy you want I'm going to have a lot of money very, very soon." Mason looked off into the distance a grin on his face. "You can divorce Jack and marry me Bella. I've always told you, I was the man you should marry. You were meant to be with me."

Bella shook her head, counting to ten in her head so she wouldn't bite his head off. It was beyond belief that while she was married to Jack, Mason would insist that she marry him instead. "You are unbelievable."

"No, everything I'm saying is quite real." Mason's grip on her waist tightened. "If you want proof that I'm telling the truth that I'll soon be a wealthy man, just stop by the town office. I'll show you."

At first Bella had no intention of being anywhere near Mason and his harebrained ideas, until suddenly a new idea came to her. Despite the fact that Mason's behavior was rude, if she played along she might discover some reason why the town council was so slow in approving Jack's Adventure Park.

"Maybe I will take you up on that offer, Mason. I would like you to show me how you plan to get all this money. When shall I stop by?"

Mason grinned like the cat who caught the canary. "Stop by tomorrow morning." He brought his face closer to hers. "I'm glad you're starting to see things my way, Bella. It won't be long now until we can be together..."

Without warning a hand grabbed Mason's shoulder.

"Get away from my wife, Mason." Jack's voice interrupted. His voice was low and threatening. His hand closed its white-knuckled grip on Mason's shoulder. "I thought we had this talk only a few weeks ago. Remember how I mentioned you'd be sorry if I ever saw you manhandling my wife again?"

"It's only a dance, Jack. Calm down." Mason face

flushed red as he stopped dancing with Bella and turned to face Jack.

Bella tensed. She wasn't prepared for a battle between the two men.

"That's where we disagree." Jack put his arm around Bella, pulling her close to his side in a protective stance. "With anyone else it would be only a dance, but with you it's more like a predator circling his prey."

"Whatever." Mason put his hands up in the air and stalked off angrily.

She sighed in relief as Mason walked away.

A scowl hovered over Jack's mouth as Mason walked off the dance floor. People around them looked at Mason and then back to Jack, puzzled expressions on their faces. Bella smiled at the crowd, hoping to help diffuse the situation.

The slow crooning of the band on stage wafted over them and Bella felt Jack's arms close around her. She hoped her husband would forget about Mason for the rest of the evening.

All she knew was that being in Jack's arms was helping her forget about the madness around her.

Being close to Jack had never felt so right. Bella's thoughts raced, waving the red flag warning, but her heart wasn't listening. Her heart was encouraging her to explore this new closeness with Jack and maybe let her husband into the deep places of her heart.

He kissed the top of her head and his grip tightened. "I don't want him near you, Bella. I hope I got through to Mason this time because if he doesn't stay away from you, I'll need to take stronger measures to protect my wife."

"I know. And I'll be okay. He's gone now." Bella glanced up at Jack glad to see his scowl slowly disappear.

Jack's embrace tightened and Bella could feel his arms tremble. He really was afraid for her -- that something could happen to her. Maybe his feelings ran deeper than she knew.

Bella loved that her husband longed to protect her. She loved being held securely in Jack's strong arms.

As the band sang about falling in love, all at once, Bella was very aware it had happened to her. She had done the very thing she'd promised herself she wouldn't do. She'd fallen in love with her husband.

All her long-winded rants to Rory, to Elle and her Dad about how she wasn't ready to get married and fall in love, were forgotten.

All she was left with was the truth that she had fallen in love with her fake husband.

What was she going to do now?

CHAPTER THIRTEEN

ella

"Good morning." Bella walked into the kitchen and saw her Dad sitting on a stool by the kitchen counter.

Mrs. Potter was bustling about making pancakes for her father. She placed a platter of freshly baked muffins on the counter.

They had returned late last night from the Founder's Day celebration. For Bella, it was a long time before she fell asleep as anxious thoughts over Jack's safety skittered across her mind.

Yawning, she walked into the kitchen.

"Mrs. Potter it smells heavenly." Bella grabbed a mug and poured herself a cup of coffee.

"I'm glad. Eat up my dear. With all those late nights

you've been working this past week, you've forgotten to eat." Jack's cook seemed to notice everything.

"I'm glad you're talking some sense into her, Mrs. Potter." Jack's low voice rumbled as he walked into the room. A shiver of warmth rolled in her belly at the sound of his voice.

She turned to him and raised one eyebrow. Her husband put one arm around her shoulders and leaned down to kiss her cheek.

"Look, I am eating." Bella pointed to her plate.

"When you get really busy, sometimes you forget to eat and need reminding sweetheart." Jack reached over and grabbed a muffin.

Bella scrunched her nose at Jack. They sounded like an old married couple. She realized just how much she longed for that to happen for her and Jack.

Her breath caught at the thought.

She took a bite of the muffin, trying to get her mind off of stray thoughts.

"Jack sit down and I'll dish out some pancakes." Mrs. Potter was about to reach for another plate, when Jack interrupted.

"Can't today, I'm afraid." Jack looked at his watch. "I'm meeting a couple of people at the mine this morning and I won't be back until late afternoon." Jack turned to look at Bella. "Come see me off?"

"Sure." Bella got up and Jack took her hand to lead her out of the kitchen to the front door.

"You'll be home today?" Jack slipped on his jacket his gaze searching hers.

"I'll be gone this morning but will be back by noon." At Bella's words, Jack's brows puckered together sharply. "I was going to stop by Dad's house. I need to find the rare books that a couple of customers have requested from my website and get them delivered." Bella tried to set his mind at ease.

"Then you'll come home?"

"Yes of course." Bella decided not to tell him that she was also stopping by the town office to talk to Mason. The night before, Jack had been overly protective about Mason dancing with her and she didn't want to cause him unnecessary anxiety. "You seem worried. Why?"

"I'm just concerned about your safety. Especially since you overheard those two men and their plans to get back at me. If they want to get to me, they won't hesitate to threaten anyone I care about." Jack took put his hands on both shoulders.

Fear shot through Bella like stray bullets pinging in every direction. She shoved the panic back down, doing her best to ease her fears.

Pushing her shoulders back, she resolved to show Jack that she was strong and unafraid. "Jack, I'll be fine. You don't need to worry about me."

Her husband pulled her close enough for her to hear his rapid heart beat. "Ah… my beauty. That's where you're wrong. I do worry about you very much. I've become very attached to you sweetheart. It would bring me too much heartache if something happened to you."

Jack pulled back for a moment to look into her eyes. Bella's heart skipped a beat as she stared into hazel eyes, darkened with emotion. His gaze moved down to her mouth, his lips came to hers and she melted. She cherished the strength of his arms around her, the feel of his rough jacket beneath her fingers.

All too soon he pulled away from her, frustration unmistakable in the set of his jaw and the storm clouds in his eyes.

"Be careful."

She wanted to help calm him. Without thinking, she reached up and with gentle hands cupped his face in her hands. "I will, I promise."

Jack reached up capturing her hands in each of his, turning them palm up. His warm lips touched the inside of each of her hands and prickles of heat burst up her arms.

Storm-filled hazel eyes fastened onto hers a little longer as if memorizing her features. He released her hands and nodded once before he quickly turned and walked out the door.

Bella stood frozen, staring at the closed door. Her heart raced with elation at the passion she heard in Jack's voice. She wanted to believe he loved her, but she realized more than likely his passion stemmed from a fierce protectiveness over those things he considered his.

Like his wife.

Heat coiled inside her belly at the memory of his passionate kisses. She wanted more of his sweet kisses. She wanted more of his strong arms encircling her. She wanted more of his heartfelt words of love.

Yet, she still had dreams of her own. Bella longed to

travel and have adventure. She longed to be a recognized leader in the field of design.

Could she have both a husband who loved her and also keep her independence? For the first time, she considered that it might be possible. She had fallen in love with her husband and desperately wanted both.

However, before they had any hope of a future together, she first needed to discover who was threatening Jack.

With a determined set to her shoulders, she hurried to get ready for her meeting with Mason.

STEPPING out of Jack's car, Bella looked up at the imposing three-story structure that took up a third of Paradise Lake's main street.

Meeting with Mason at the town office, was the last thing she wanted to do, and yet she was desperate to learn more about why the town council was so slow in approving Jack's project.

Dark storm clouds above forewarned of a coming storm, an echo of the gloomy shadows inside of her. As she pulled the glass door open, she set her jaw, determined to do whatever it took to get the answers she needed.

"Bella. It's a surprise to see you here." Vonda, a grey haired woman in her fifties, peered up at her with sharp eyes. "I used to run into you like clockwork at the Library, but I don't see you there anymore. I hear your quite busy working on a design project for Jack Stevenson."

Bella was fairly certain Vonda was searching for more

fodder for the gossip mill. The town office secretary managed not only those who worked in the building, but had also been a source of information for many people in their small town.

"Yes, I've been designing Jack's Adventure Park. It's almost ready to go and we're excited."

"Well, you've been busy then. Molly at the Library told me you designed their website. You did an incredible job." She put a hand under her chin a bright smile on her face.

"Thanks Vonda. I love adding color and creating fun designs."

"Well it needed it. We could use a facelift on our website too. I'll mention your work to Mayor Rainey." Bella smiled and nodded at her words of praise. "Also, a belated congratulations on your wedding to Jack."

Bella was sure she would hardly get a word in edgewise if she didn't start talking. She wasn't interested in sharing more details than necessary about her life, for fear of feeding the local gossips. "Thanks Vonda. Hey I was wondering if Mason is in his office this morning? I have an appointment."

A furrow formed between Vonda's brows and disappointment etched her features. She sighed and looked down at her computer, clicking her mouse until she got the right webpage.

"Yes, of course. Give me a moment and I'll check." She picked up the phone to buzz him. "Bella Stevenson to see you. All right, I'll send her in."

Bella followed Vonda down the hallway and knocked on a large oak door. She looked around to see a large room filled with office workers, each hard at work at their cubicles.

"Bella, you're here. Come on in." Mason opened his office door and with his hand on her shoulder walked her inside. Bella had to stifle the urge to shake his hand off her shoulder as he led her to a soft chair in front of his desk.

She forced herself to smile. "You sound surprised. Of course I'm here and eager to hear more details about what you told me at the dance last night."

Mason sat behind his desk, elbows on his desk and fingers steepled. His eyes glittered, like a proud peacock with its feathers on display for people to walk by and admire.

"Of course. I'm glad you're finally willing to see things my way, Bella." Mason's cocky attitude made her want to run out of the room, but she forced herself to stay put.

He opened a desk drawer and pulled out some documents, placing them in front of her. "I promised to show you how I will soon be rich Bella, and there it is." He pointed to a document that displayed a graph showing a future forecast of increasing profit.

"This looks like a map of Paradise Lake with large condos along the lakefront."

"It is. That's where the next big wave of profit is. Get ready for the new future of Paradise Lake. A future I'm proud to be part of along with a few other investors." Mason eyes glittered, until Bella was sure she could see dollar signs in his pupils.

"I thought condos being built along the lakefront were only rumors."

"No, this is very real." Mason's pointed to the map.

Bella got a closer look at the map. "This spot along the beach looks like it's really close to Jack's land where he wants to build the Adventure Park."

"Yes, sadly that row of condominiums will really decrease Jack's view of the lake and surrounding mountains. It will also negatively affect his property value." He spoke the words carelessly, as if none of it mattered. "Jack will be out of luck and likely won't get the approval he needs from the town to build his adventure park."

Bella stiffened as anger turned her blood to hot molten lava. Mason and those other investors were doing this deliberately to try to ruin Jack.

She was just about to give him a piece of her mind, when there was a loud knock on his office door.

Mason stood to open the door. A tall, slender blonde stood there in a short sweater dress that emphasized every curve in her body. Bella recognized her as the same woman who had stopped by their product table and insulted Jack at the Founder's Day celebration.

Suddenly Bella's thoughts went in a different direction. Mason and the Wolffe brothers weren't above using their office assistant to try to derail Jack's project. It was obvious by building their condos that they were hindering Jack's goals for the Adventure Park.

Were there more secrets Mason was hiding?

"Tiffany, can't you see I'm busy? What is it?" Mason's tone was filled with irritation.

"You need to come with me and talk to this man. He's quite upset." Tiffany's high-pitched voice sounded more like a whine.

"All right, I'll talk to him." Mason turned and turning to Bella he spoke quickly, "I'll be back in just a moment."

"Of course." Bella gave him a small smile and he left the office. As soon as Mason was gone, Bella took out her smartphone and walked around his desk. Aware that Mason could return at any moment, she needed to work fast.

Opening drawers she pulled out a few files and quickly scanned through them, not finding anything important.

She went through the next drawer and still there was nothing. The last drawer she didn't think there was anything of consequence, but when she skimmed her fingers along the bottom of the drawer, they caught a small ribbon. Tugging on the ribbon, she pulled until a wooden board pulled up.

Bella expelled a breath when she saw the secret compartment. There were a bunch of documents there.

For once, Bella was glad for Mason's aversion to using digital methods to store important documents. Ever since High School, he kept a paper trail and it looked like today was her lucky day.

With hurried movements Bella turned the pages, scanning to see if there was anything important.

The first file showed information on Senator Ivan Wolffe. Scanning through the documents she read descriptions of the new condominiums that were to be built.

Further notes on the documents stated that funding for the project would be provided by SOS Group, with a handwritten note that someone tried to cross out. She looked closer and saw the words, seeing where the Senator was receiving funding for this project.

Bella took out her smartphone and began taking pictures of all the documents so she could show Jack.

As she continued through the file, she found pictures of Senator Wolffe with his brothers Bert and Bart taken with some men and women she didn't recognize. Next, there was a map of the United States, and some cities in different states were circled in red. There were addresses written in red ink beside each location.

Another document had pictures and names of two different men with notes beside them of each of their expertise. The words written beside the first name was chemicals, and beside the other man's name was written homemade bombs.

Swallowing back fear, Bella grabbed her smartphone and started snapping pictures of the documents. She hurried to put all the documents back and slid the wooden board into place and placed the rest of the files on top of it before closing the drawer.

She had just slipped her smartphone into her pocket, when Mason opened the door. One eyebrow raised in question before he asked. "See anything interesting?"

Bella face flushed and she squirmed a little at being caught standing so near his desk. She was thankful he hadn't opened the door a minute sooner. Her heart was still racing with fear from all that she'd just discovered.

Spotting a picture on his desk, she picked it up. "I was just admiring your photo with your little sister." Bella remembered Mason's little sister from when she would hang around with them in High School.

"Well that was taken a few summers ago. But, yes I like to keep that on my desk to remind myself to call her once in awhile." Mason walked over to Bella taking the picture out of her hands putting it back on his desk. "But, back to our previous conversation. What do you think of the condos?"

"They look like they are designed well, but I don't believe these large condos should be built so near Jack's land." Bella walked to the other side of his desk her brows furrowed together in frustration at the thought.

"Ha, that's a laugh. If it ruins his view and property value, then I think that's good. There's only one of us that needs to be taken down a peg or two, and it ain't me."

Bella suddenly remembered the two men talking in the hallway, during the Founder's Day celebration. One man had spoken those same words about Jack.

It was him.

She recognized his voice. Mason was one of the men who had threatened Jack.

Swaying a little she leaned against Mason's desk, feeling the blood drain away from her face.

"Are you okay? You don't look well." Mason stepped away from her.

Bella looked up at him suddenly seeing her ex-boyfriend for the first-time as a horrible person who would harm others to reach his own goals. She couldn't believe he was part of this… terrible plot. Just the sight of him made her sick.

"You're right. I'm suddenly not feeling well. I'm going to head home." She walked to the office door her hand on the doorknob before she turned around. "I need to say this. It's not okay to ruin someone else's life just to make your own better no matter how much money you stand to gain from it."

"Well, that's where we disagree Bella." Mason laughed, crossing his arms over his chest.

She closed the door and hurried out of the town office, not even pausing to say goodbye to Vonda. It was only as Bella got into her car that she let out the breath she'd been holding.

Her heart raced as she leaned her head against the steering wheel. She needed to get home to Jack. She needed to tell him what she'd learned.

All of a sudden, her phone rang. "Bella, there's been a change of plans. Meet me at the hospital as soon as you can." Jack's voice sounded harried.

"Why? Did something happen to my Dad?" She sat up and gripped the steering wheel her knuckles turning white.

"No. Your Dad's fine." At Jack's words, Bella sank back against her seat in relief. She really wouldn't have been able to handle her Dad going back into the hospital again.

"It's Elle. She's had her baby." She heard Jack's chuckle at the other end of the phone line. Elle and Adam had their baby. Excited at the prospect of seeing the new little one, she started the car.

"I'll be there as soon as I can." Bella hung up her phone and started driving to the hospital. As she parked the car in the hospital parking lot, she realized that her talk with Jack about what she'd discovered today, would need to be put on hold until later.

Bella hurried into the hospital.

Seeing Elle's name on one of the doors in the maternity wing, she pushed it open only to see the Stevenson family laughing and carrying on.

Eliza Stevenson held the swaddled baby close to her heart, her eyes bright and smile beaming. Granddad and Grandmom sat on the other side, their smiles radiant at the sight of their first great-grandchild.

Gabe, Luke and Zach were all standing on the opposite side of the room next to Adam, smiling like the proud uncles they were.

"Congratulations Elle and Adam. This is so exciting." Bella gave Elle and Adam each a little hug before she stood beside Jack. Her husband pulled her close to his side.

"Thanks Bella. We couldn't be more excited that our son is finally here."

Elle looked up at Adam who leaned down and kissed her forehead.

"He's perfect, Elle." Bella looked at the beautiful sleeping baby, then back at Elle whose face lit up with pride.

"Here, it's your turn to hold him." Eliza stood to her feet and walked over to Bella, gently transferring the baby into her arms.

Tears formed in her eyes and one slid down her cheek as she stared at the tiny baby boy. A tiny tuft of dark blonde hair curled at the top of his head. His tiny nose and perfect little mouth gave him the look of a little angel.

Bella slipped one finger under his fingers, which the tiny boy grabbed onto with a tight grip. "I'm in love with this little one." She looked at Elle and then up at Jack.

His eyes were shuttered over, but she could see a softening in his hazel eyes. Elle sat up farther on the bed and whispered something to Adam who nodded.

Looking back at Bella and Jack, Elle asked, "Adam and I have something to ask you two."

Bella could feel Jack's hand tense on her shoulder.

"Would the two of you be willing to be little Daniel Adam's godparents?" Elle and Adam looked at them a hopeful smile on their faces.

Bella looked up at Jack, a silent question in his hooded gaze. She nodded at him, her smile wide and welcoming.

"We'd be honored." Jack swallowed convulsively as he studied his brother and sister-in-law.

Bella turned to give the baby to Jack.

Hesitantly Jack took the tiny bundle into his arms. A pained expression crossed her husband's face that lasted only a moment as he looked down at the baby boy in his arms. He held the infant only for a moment before passing the baby back to his mama.

"We're very happy for you both. We'll come visit again, but Bella and I need to leave as we have other commitments today." Jack kissed Elle on the cheek and gave Adam a hug, leaving Bella to do the same before she followed him out of the hospital room.

Bella had to hurry to keep up with her husband. It was pouring rain as they stepped out of the hospital.

"Jack, why did we need to leave so suddenly? Is something troubling you? Talk to me Jack. Help me understand." Bella stood by the door out of the rain.

Her husband looked at her a haunted look reflected in his eyes. "We'll talk when we get home."

Bella nodded and followed after him, wondering what was going on with Jack. Driving home, all she could think about was how she wished Jack would trust her enough to tell her what troubled him.

He said they would talk at home. Bella really hoped this time he would open up and let her into his world.

CHAPTER FOURTEEN

ack

RAIN PELTED the truck's windshield as Jack drove up the hill to his home.

His thoughts whirled in so many directions.

Bella had asked what troubled him. There were many things, too many to mention. He didn't even know where to start.

He parked his truck and waited in the rain as Bella parked her car. Opening her door, he held her hand and together they ran into the house.

Jack helped Bella out of her jacket first before he removed his own.

Ben was waiting for them. "Mrs. Potter said to tell you,

she has hot tea and light snacks waiting for you in the kitchen."

"Thank you Ben. We'll change into dry clothes first, but would you ask her to bring tea into the Conservatory?" Jack asked as he hung up their wet jackets.

"Of course." Ben hurried away.

"Since, I'm feeling like a drowned cat I'm going to take a moment to shower and get into some dry clothes." Bella wiped water away from her face as it dripped down her cheeks.

Jack brushed her wet hair away from her forehead. "I'll do the same. Meet me in the Conservatory?"

"Sure." Bella hurried down the hallway to her room.

Jack watched her walk away, thinking she looked adorable.

As he took a warm shower and changed into dry clothes, the picture of Bella holding Adam and Elle's baby was vivid in his thoughts. She'd looked so beautiful holding their son. Bella would make an amazing mother someday.

He was already jealous of the man who would someday win Bella's heart and have a family with her.

A familiar heartache formed as he remembered the death of his wife and unborn son. For someone like him, he didn't deserve a second chance.

Walking into the Conservatory, Jack breathed deep the familiar scent of roses. He stood there for a moment, letting the pitter-patter of rain falling on the glass ceiling above soothe his troubled mind.

As soon as he sat in the familiar soft chair, he heard the door open.

With a hooded gaze, he watched Bella walk toward him. Dressed in simple jeans and light pink sweater she was beautiful. Her thick brown hair hung down her back in waves, swaying gently with her hips as she walked toward him.

Just being in the same room as his wife, made him yearn to kiss her and hold her close. He wondered if Bella knew the effect she had on him.

His wife sat beside him on the cushioned love seat. The scent of lavender wafted up his nose and he moved closer.

"It's so peaceful here." Bella leaned back and put her feet up, turning to look at him.

"Yeah. It's a good place to think." Jack closed his eyes for a minute and breathed in deep.

Hearing the clink of cups, Bella stood to her feet. "Thank you Mrs. Potter. This smells wonderful."

Jack turned to nod his thanks just before his housekeeper turned and walked out of the room. Bella handed him a cup of tea and she sat down holding her cup close to her chest.

"Were you surprised today when Adam and Elle asked the two of us to be baby Daniel's godparents?" Bella sipped her tea, her brown eyes peering at him over the rim.

"Yeah. I wasn't expecting that." A mixture of emotions welled up inside him.

"Me too. I've never seen myself as anyone's godparent. It seems like a very big responsibility." Bella sipped her tea for a moment, pausing before she continued. "It's overwhelming but it's also an honor to help guide a tiny human being to adulthood."

Jack only nodded. She summed up so much of how he felt about his new role in his nephew's life.

"Do you think you'll want a child of your own someday?"

Jack turned to her, angsty feelings rising to the surface. "I already had a son and he died. I don't think I can do that again."

Bella winced and Jack expelled a breath. "Sorry, that came out harsher than I intended. Forgive me?"

"I do forgive you Jack. I really wish you would tell me more of what happened years ago." Bella put her teacup down and moved closer to him, slipping her small hand in his.

He squeezed her hand like it was his lifeline.

How could he talk about this with Bella? He'd only allowed himself one day a year to remember and mourn, and the rest of the time he pushed down all memories of his first wife and their unborn son.

Maybe it was time he told her. If he finally told her all of it, maybe it would help her realize how impossible it was for them to consider any sort of future together.

"Elin and I met in college. She was usually the life of any party and there were a lot of those in my wild college days." Jack paused a moment looking at the plants as he remembered.

"She was beautiful and full of life. After a whirlwind romance, we eloped in Las Vegas. I really thought she loved me like I loved her, but I didn't discover how fickle her love really was until after we were married." He looked at Bella who sat there quietly listening. Her big brown eyes were full of acceptance and understanding.

Jack continued, his voice monotone. "After we married, I learned how obsessed she was with how she appeared to others. It wasn't until a year had gone by, that I found out about the gambling debts. And it was right around that time when debt collectors started coming to the door."

He shifted uncomfortably as jarring memories invaded his thoughts. "Of course I paid them off, but she really hated it when I set much lower limits on her charge cards and bank accounts. She started to be angry all the time and began going on all these diets, obsessing about her appearance. The one time I mentioned having children, she shut me down and told me there was no way she was going to have stretch marks and ruin her body to have a child. So I left it alone and we didn't talk about it again."

He expelled a long breath and shook his head remembering. "Then she caught a cold and forgot to take the pills she was on to prevent pregnancy. We found out three weeks later, she was pregnant. She was so angry after that. I told her it would be okay. I told her I would plan my schedule so I could stay home to help her throughout the pregnancy. I was thrilled to have a child, but I couldn't share my happiness with my wife." His voice was unsteady to his own ears. "I did everything I could to help her, but it wasn't enough."

Jack ran a shaky hand through his hair. "By the time she was five months pregnant, Elin was stir crazy and asked her cousin to stay with her. When her cousin arrived, I realized I wasn't needed. So when your Dad asked me to meet him at the science fair, I went."

Bella sighed and spoke, "That was the weekend I was kidnapped and you saved me."

"Yes, but by doing so I received a scar so hideous that when I returned home, my own wife couldn't stand the sight of me."

Bella gasped. Her eyes widened and eyebrows puckered together in anger. "Then she didn't deserve you."

Jack let out the barest of smiles at his wife's defense of him. He didn't deserve it, but he appreciated it all the same.

"When you got home, that's when she left you?" Bella put her hand to her mouth and shook her head.

"Yes. She took one look at me and screamed." Jack rubbed the back of his neck. "I tried to hold her to help calm her down, but she yelled at me to get away. She didn't want me touching her at all. It was the next day when I came home from the office that I saw the hand-written note on the kitchen counter.

His voice shook slightly as he continued, "In the note she'd written, "I can't look at you and see your face day after day, Jack. I mean before you looked sort of like a rugged modern-day Tarzan, which I liked. But now, you look awful. You look horrible. You look beastly. I just can't stay with you… not now."

"That's horrible. How could she be so cruel?" Bella squeezed his hand.

Memories that had haunted Jack for years came crashing down on him. He let go of her hand and leaned his elbows on his knees, his head in his hands. "A policeman came to the door late that night, to tell me that my wife and unborn son had been killed instantly in a head-on collision."

Jack's shoulders shook as sobs ripped through him.

Bella put her arm around his shoulder and leaned close. "Let all the pain out, Jack. You need to grieve. You must have loved your wife and unborn son very much."

Suddenly he turned, venting his anger and grief. "No, I didn't love Elin like I should have. Don't you see? I didn't love and take care of my family as I should have. That's why I deserved Elin's hatred. I deserved the scar. I deserved to have my son die."

"No, that's not true Jack. Why would you say such a thing?"

"Because, I've been selfish and uncaring for so long that it's finally coming back around like I deserve."

"Jack that's not…" He interrupted her.

"It is true." In his mind, everything was coming full circle and he was finally getting what he deserved. "I left my father alone to deal with the stress of his business partner's betrayal, which cost my Dad his life. I brought shame on my mom, brothers and grandparents because of my heavy drinking and partying in college. I didn't understand how crazy the pregnancy was making my wife as well as not realizing how much the scar on my face would shock her. I failed my family, I failed my wife and I failed my unborn son."

He stood up and paced back and forth between the rose bushes that lined the far wall of the conservatory. "If hindsight gives you twenty-twenty vision, then I finally see perfectly. If I'd been a better man, most likely none of this would've happened. And my son would not have died."

Bella stood to her feet and walked toward him. He stopped when he saw the tears that streamed down her cheeks. He stood rigid as she reached her arms around him to embrace him.

"I'm so sorry, Jack." She pulled back, big brown eyes searching his. "I'm sorry for every loss. I'm sorry for every heartache. I'm sorry for all the pain you went through. But, you don't need to be alone any longer. We can get through this together."

Jack's hazel eyes glittered as he stepped out of her embrace. His skin had drawn tight over his features, twisting the thick scar that slashed across his face. He looked fierce. "Now that you've got a good look at the ugly beast inside me Bella… I'm sure you can see why I've closed myself off to most of the rest of the world. Do you really think anyone — any woman — would truly want to be bonded in marriage to a beast like me?"

Crossing his arms in front of him, his eyes cold, demanding an answer. Jack needed her to see and accept the truth about himself as he saw it.

Bella flinched at his callous words, but he needed to say it.

He wanted honesty between them. Far better that he hear that his wife hated him than repeat the same mistake he made with Elin.

Yet, fear coiled in his belly that she would reject him outright.

JARRED by her husband's words, for a moment she stood frozen. The impact of his traumatic story had shaken her.

Until this moment, Bella hadn't understood how much pain and anger Jack held inside from all he'd gone through.

As her husband shared his story of pain and heartache, she wept. Bella stood motionless, a new awareness dawning. Fear of getting close to another woman and going through deep pain was what held him back from loving again. He was afraid he would be rejected once more.

Suddenly, everything became clear. It was as if a fog had been removed, and for the first time she could see.

"Jack," She breathed his name, stepping close to him. Bella reached up, her fingertips gently tracing the deep scar that ran vertically on the right side of his face, from brow to jaw. He trembled under her touch but didn't move away. She traced the length of the scar. Finding courage, Bella stood on tiptoe, stretching up to him, and placed her lips on the deepest part of his scar.

Jack tightened his hands on her shoulders and she felt his body shudder against her. "Bella... don't."

She ignored him.

Instead, his wife trailed her lips along the ridge of marred flesh.

"Your scars are part of who you are, Jack," she whispered. "I used to notice them more, but since you married me that changed." She was so close, their breath mingled as one. "Now, all I see is a man who is a loving son and brother and a kind-hearted and protective husband. I see the face of the man I love."

Bella stepped back a little ways, her hands trembling as

they rested lightly on his muscled forearms. She looked away for a moment, worried over Jack's reaction to her words of love.

Finally she lifted her gaze to meet his.

A haunted look lingered in Jack's eyes. His hazel eyes, darkened to a deep brown as he reached his hands up to her shoulders his fingers gently touching the curve of her neck. His fingertips toyed with her hair and he pulled her close.

He leaned his forehead against hers, tremors shaking his body as he expelled a long breath. "I don't deserve your love, Bella. You should run as far away from me as possible. I'm too broken inside."

Shaking her head she was about to speak when Jack cupped her face in his hands, looking deeply into her eyes. "You are all that is beautiful and lovely. I'm worried if you stay with me, I'll end up ruining you. There's too much pain inside me. Too much hurt."

"No, you won't ruin me. You can heal, Jack. I think you just need time to let go of the past, forgive yourself and believe in yourself again." Bella touched his cheek in a gentle caress.

"I don't know how."

"I'm here for you, Jack. We'll do this together." Her heart ached for him and for all that he'd suffered.

A shuttered look passed over his eyes.

He looked away for a moment and then down at her. With his jaw set in determination, he seemed to come to a decision.

"I can't do this to you, Bella. I can't dump all my messes and failures onto you. I can't cause you that kind of pain."

Jack stared at her a little longer before he suddenly leaned down to whisper. "But, I'm selfish and need one last kiss." His lips found hers with an intensity that shocked Bella.

Her arms slipped around his neck, her legs trembled and went weak as he deepened their kiss.

Without warning, he stepped away and out of her embrace.

His whispered words were hurried, "Bella, don't think of me. Don't dream of me. Don't love me. I'm just no good for you." Jack leaned over her hands, kissing each one before he spun on his heel and left the room.

Bella stood there stunned.

What just happened?

One moment he was sharing the deepest part of his heart and the next moment he was hurrying out of the room. Away from her.

Shivering suddenly, she ran her hands along her arms.

Jack had run away from her.

No, it wasn't her that he was running away from. Jack was desperate to get away from what he saw as his own failures, mistakes and heartache.

Was there some deeper part of him that she had failed to understand?

I need to find the answers. I need to know the deepest part of his heart. Tomorrow morning when Jack leaves for the silver mine, I know just where to look.

CHAPTER FIFTEEN

ella

"I'LL JUST HAVE coffee this morning, Mrs. Potter. I'm not very hungry." Bella had already been awake for hours, tossing and turning most of the night.

As she watched Mrs. Potter make a fresh pot of coffee and mix a batter for muffins, her brows puckered in worry over Jack.

Knots had formed in her stomach and kept her awake most of the night. Bella rehearsed her conversation with Jack over and over.

What had gone wrong?

The evening that had started so well, ended so poorly.

Jack had shared his deepest heartache and pain with her.

She'd never seen him so vulnerable. His shame, regret

and failures clung to him like a second skin. After all these years, he still carried misplaced responsibility for his father's death and for the loss of his wife and unborn son.

Jack's words from last night made her tremble. *I didn't love Elin like I should have. Don't you see? I didn't love and take care of my family as I should have. That's why I deserved Elin's hatred. I deserved the scar. I deserved to have my son die.*

She couldn't shake the sense that Jack had been pushing her away. That he was trying to tell her goodbye.

But, Bella was just as determined not to let her husband go without a fight.

She swallowed the rest of her coffee and stood to her feet.

"Thanks for the coffee." Bella quickly washed her cup setting it to dry in the dish rack.

"You're welcome. Come back later for muffins." Mrs. Potter waved her off and Bella hurried out of the kitchen and down the hallway to the West Wing.

Today she decided, she was going to uncover her husband's secrets.

If it meant she had to go against her husband's express wishes, she would. When she reached the last door on the left, she looked behind her and seeing no one, she walked inside.

This was her husband's bedroom.

The large room looked masculine with its blue and grey colors on the walls and furniture.

Her hand shook as she opened the top drawer.

It's not too late. You can stop this madness now. You don't need to find the key to go into that secret room.

The voice in her head, tried to stop her. This was the

only way she could learn the real truth before it was too late. Last night it sounded like her husband was withdrawing. She couldn't just sit back and let him leave.

Their relationship was too important to leave to chance.

Bella searched through his dresser drawers, but found nothing. Looking around the room she spotted two nightstands, one on either side of the large king size bed.

Mesmerized she stood motionless, staring at the bed.

Heat rose from her neck to her cheeks as she imagined what it would be like to be a real wife to Jack. He could picture being held in his arms every night and them loving each other.

Bella stop thinking about that. Making this a real marriage wasn't part of your agreement with Jack.

She shook her head to chase away the images popping up in her imagination.

As she walked toward the nightstand she saw a phone, a lamp and a picture. As she bent over to see the picture clearly, she realized it was a picture of her and Jack at the theme park in Paris. It was a picture of them smiling at each other, Jack's arm was around her waist and she had sparkles in their eyes.

Memories of that day brought a warm glow of happiness to Bella.

Why would he keep this picture of the two of them by his bedside?

A tiny spark of hope ignited in Bella. Maybe Jack cared for her more than she realized.

Opening the drawer to the nightstand she saw a couple

pens, a notebook and a TV remote. Looking farther back she spotted a ring of three keys.

Her hand shook a little as she grabbed the keys.

Closing the drawer quickly, she hurried out of Jack's bedroom and out into the hallway.

All was quiet with no one in sight.

She walked toward the door to the secret room, slipped the key in the doorknob and opened the door.

Hurrying inside, she pushed the door closed and switched on the light.

Bella held her breath and looked around.

Being in this room was like standing inside a sacred chamber for the dead.

On one wall were large pictures of Jack with his father. They were fishing together, playing baseball together and there was a picture of his father's arms around Jack when he was around thirteen.

The next wall held large black and white pictures of a tiny baby in the womb. Bella realized the pictures must have been the sonogram that was taken when Jack's wife was pregnant with their son. Next to those pictures, was one small picture of his first wife in the late stages of pregnancy.

As she looked down at the set of shelves below the pictures, she saw the handwritten note that Jack's pregnant wife wrote before she left. It had been torn up and haphazardly pieced together.

Bella read those terrible words. *I can't look at you and see your face day after day, Jack. I mean before you looked sort of like a rugged modern-day Tarzan, which I liked. But now, you look awful. You look horrible. You look beastly. I just can't stay with you. Not now.*

Her hands shook and she dropped the note.

Why would Jack hold onto these stinging words of rejection? With a heavy heart, she continued to look around the room.

On the opposite wall were pictures of Jack standing in the middle of his mom and four brothers, with his arms around their shoulders. From Jack's lopsided smile and bloodshot eyes, he looked like he might have had a little too much to drink before this picture was taken.

It was almost as if this room was Jack's burial chamber of all that he'd lost.

To Bella, it seemed like her husband kept all the things in this room as a reminder of all his failures and regrets.

Jack believed he didn't deserve love because of all he'd done wrong.

He didn't feel worthy enough to be forgiven.

He didn't feel worthy enough to hope for a new beginning.

He didn't feel worthy enough to be loved again.

A tear slipped down Bella's cheek for all the ways Jack had punished himself over the years.

Spying the baby crib and rocking chair over in the corner, she walked toward it and sat down. Her hands twisted together and white-hot pain coursed through her veins and she felt Jack's pain as if it were her own.

The pictures that hung on the wall and the empty crib beside her was proof of that. As her gaze switched to the small table beside her, she noticed a small audio player.

Curious, she pressed the play button.

When the popular children's song, *Lullaby* by Johannes

Brahms, began to play, she smiled softly at Jack's choice in music.

Memories surfaced of her father playing this song and singing the words softly to her every night as a small child. Tears trickled down her cheeks as the words to the first verse flitted through her mind.

Lullaby, and good night, with roses bedight,
With lilies overspread is my baby's wee bed.
Lay thee down now and rest, may thy slumber be blessed.
Lay thee down now and rest, may thy slumber be blessed.

THE GENTLE LULLING of this song made her feel safe and loved. It always reminded Bella of her Dad's love.

But she wondered what thoughts went through Jack's head when he heard this song? Did he remember the son he lost?

She stopped rocking as a new revelation hit her. Jack had named his dog, Brahms.

He had told her Brahms was now four years old. Did he name his dog after the composer of the children's Lullaby? Did he get the dog for his soon-to-be born son?

Bella was pondering all these things when suddenly the door opened wide and Jack burst inside.

Her husband stood before her, his eyes wide with accusation. "Bella, what are you doing in here?"

Brahms was by his side and lay down at the low growl he heard from his master's voice. For a moment, Bella stared at him stunned that he was home and standing in front of her.

She clicked the audio player off and stood to her feet.

Her hands trembled and she wiped them on her jeans. "Ah, I just…"

Jack stopped her mid-sentence. "Didn't I make it clear to you that this was the one room in the house I didn't want you to enter?"

Anger flashed in his unflinching gaze.

It seemed she had miscalculated on how upset Jack would be at her for invading his private space.

"Yes, you did make it clear. And I'm sorry Jack for not respecting your wishes." Bella wiped the tears quickly away from her cheeks.

Jack watched her, his eyes stormy and his shoulders stiff and resolute. A tick in the rigid set of his jaw, revealed his anger.

Bella shifted and bravely stepped closer to Jack, placing her hand on his arm. "Forgive me Jack?"

Her husband's gaze was cold and steady, but his eyes flickered at her apology. "Let's get out of here."

With hurried steps, she walked ahead of her husband and into the hallway and waited. He walked out, the furrow between his brows revealed his simmering anger.

Bella shifted nervously, not knowing what else to say to Jack. She'd never seen him this angry. He stared at her without saying a word. Swallowing nervously, she remembered the key. She pulled it out of her pocket and handed it to him.

He took the key and slipped it into his pocket. "I've got to get back."

"But you just got home."

"I came home to let you know there was an explosion at the mine."

Bella's eyes flew open wide.

He ran a hand through his hair. "No one was killed, but a couple of my men were hurt. I've called the ambulance and they should be here soon."

Bella expelled the breath she'd been holding.

"I just wanted to let you know, so you wouldn't worry. Now, I need to hurry and get back. You'll be safe here with Ben and Mrs. Potter. We'll talk when I get back." Her husband nodded at her and hurried away.

She stood there in the empty hallway for a moment longer, before she turned and walked into the Conservatory. So many mixed emotions warred inside her.

Bella paced through the greenery in the conservatory, her thoughts flitting back and forth between what she'd learned about her husband in that secret room to the displeasure he'd shown at finding her there.

Waves of guilt rolled over her. She'd let her impulsive nature guide her decisions and it had landed her in hot water with her husband. Even though she'd apologized, Jack had been too upset with her to forgive her.

The reason he'd come back to the house, was to tell her about the explosion in the mine. Jack wanted to let her know, so she wouldn't hear about it from someone else, and worry. She was grateful that he wanted to protect her.

Since meeting with Mason, she realized just how important that was. Bella realized she still hadn't told Jack about the documents she'd found in Mason's office. More than likely what she discovered was related to the explosion at the mine.

She hurried out of the conservatory to the entryway of the house. Slipping on a light jacket and comfortable walking shoes she was ready to go.

Ben passed her in his hurry to the kitchen.

"Ben, can I ask for a favor?"

"Of course, Mrs. Stevenson."

"Did Jack tell you there was an explosion at the mine?"

"Yes, I've been organizing the ambulance and sending extra help."

She nodded. "Good. Well I just wanted to ask if you could let Mrs. Potter know that I'm going to see Jack at the mine? I think I have an idea who might be responsible for the blast and I need to let Jack know. I'll be back in awhile." Bella pulled the sleeves down on her jacket.

"You shouldn't be going there. Jack won't like it. It's not safe, especially not today." Ben's brows puckered in worry.

"I appreciate your concern, but it's critical that I tell Jack. He will understand after I explain."

"I don't like you being out there where it's not safe, Mrs. Stevenson." Ben's mouth formed a grimace, his brows puckered in worry.

Bella touched his arm lightly. "I really appreciate your concern Ben, but I'll be fine. I can take care of myself."

She smiled at Jack's assistant and opened the door.

A cool brisk wind blew into her face and tugged at her coat as she stepped outside. She zipped her jacket up to her neck.

Hurrying toward the shed she found the four-wheeler

her and Jack used the last time they'd gone to the mine. Turning it on, she drove the ATV out of the shed and along the trail that led to the mine.

Reaching the mine, she parked the ATV and hurried toward the entrance. Many miners stood outside along with the ambulance and EMTs.

Seeing Jack's mining supervisor, she walked toward him. "Mike, do you know where I can find Jack?"

"I do, but it's really not safe for you here Mrs. Stevenson. You should just go back home. You can talk to your husband when he gets home." Mike's large body stood like a fortress, guarding the mine's entrance.

"I appreciate that you're trying to protect me Mike, but it's critical that I talk to Jack."

"Mrs. Stevenson that's not a good idea…"

"Would it help if I told you I need to talk to Jack because I think I have an idea who is responsible for the explosion in the mine?" Bella smiled and watched Mike's eyes grow wide in understanding.

Jack's foreman nodded. "Follow me. He's over this way."

Bella had to step around chunks of heavy rocks and debris as they made their way to the back of the mine. They followed the path that Jack had taken her last time she'd been here.

A loud jarring sound of steel against rock only got louder as they rounded the corner. She looked up to see Jack swinging the pickaxe over his shoulder, hitting the solid rock with pieces flying through the air in every direction.

Mike motioned for her to stay back. Bella waited as Mike approached Jack.

Her husband stopped swinging and as his foreman pointed in her direction, Jack stared at her, his eyes cold and hard.

The foreman walked away in a hurry.

As she took in Jack's livid expression, she wanted to turn back and run the other way. She stood frozen as her husband walked slowly toward her.

His low growl could have curdled milk. "What are you doing here? I thought I told you to stay at home where it was safe."

Bella's felt the blood drain from her face at his harsh words. Despite his gruffness, Bella stood still and faced him.

"But I have something important to tell you Jack." He just crossed his arms and stared at her. Bella rubbed her arms in an effort to warm herself from the abrupt chill from his frostiness.

She needed to apologize again. "I'm sorry I went into your secret room Jack. It was an impulsive idea that I shouldn't have acted on. I hope you will forgive me."

Still he did not move. "I know you're sorry, Bella. But, I need more time. I'm not ready to talk about it yet." Jack expelled a frustrated sigh.

Bella thought she'd try again. "But it's important that I tell you…"

"Not now, Bella. Can't you see I'm not ready to talk about this yet? Go back home. We'll talk later."

Bella stiffened her back as her husband spun on his heel and just as quickly went back to work.

Frustrated by her stubborn husband, Bella watched him for a few moments longer before turning to leave.

Her mind was preoccupied with Jack's coldness towards her. *He didn't even listen to me. He just pushed me away like a child needing to go home.*

Bella sighed irritated with her husband. He never did say he forgave her. *Stop complaining Bella. It's partly your fault Jack is in such a foul mood. You shouldn't have gone behind his back.*

Expelling a long breath, she hardly noticed where she was going.

The mine was dark as she walked. Her thoughts were a muddle and she was unsure which tunnel would take her back to the mine's entrance.

Bella thought she could hear voices down one of the tunnels, so she turned in that direction.

She'd only taken a few steps, when suddenly strong arms grabbed her from behind holding her still. As she began to scream a hand covered her mouth, muffling her cries for help.

Panic — cold and heavy — landed at the bottom of Bella's stomach.

A crack, cold and tiny, suddenly got bigger in the pit of her belly and coiled its way up, leaving a trail of ice. It was like a plumber's snake slithered through her insides, sucking up all the blood.

Memories assaulted her. She'd faced this terror years ago with the kidnappers.

Determined not to let this happen to her a second time, she kicked at his legs, in a desperate attempt to get away from the man. It was no use. His hold on her was like an iron grip.

Bella didn't know how far he dragged her against her will. After a very long time, they reached a place in the mine where it was completely dark with no light.

She could hardly breathe.

Her captor forced her to sit down. She was seated on the edge of a big rock but scrambled to get away. He caught her and held her tight while he tied ropes around her wrists and placed a gag over her mouth. She managed to kick him, but he soon tied her feet too.

It was only when she was all tied up, that her captor began to speak.

It was completely dark, so she couldn't see his face.

"Bella, how good of you to join me here." To her horror, Mason's grating voice broke through the silence. "I know you must be surprised to hear my voice. As much as I'd dearly love to see your face right now, I won't turn on the flashlight. Don't want anyone to find you, I'm sure you understand."

Anger sizzled in Bella and her nostrils flared as she tried to yell at him.

"Sorry, with that gag on, I can't understand a word you're saying, Bella." Mason laughed in his usual overbearing way.

Fear was causing her breaths to become more rapid and shallow. She forced herself to slow down her breathing so she wouldn't pass out. She was convinced Mason was completely mad. Why did he hope to gain by holding her hostage?

Mason stopped his pacing and stood beside her once

again. "You might be wondering why I would drag you deep into the mine where no one can find you. Well, I'll tell you."

He paused and continued, "I'm tired of Jack taking everything that should be mine. He has enough money to do whatever he likes, he's won over the good opinion of many of the Town Council members and most of all he married you — the girl I had planned to marry."

Bella whispered that she wouldn't have him as her husband even if he begged, but she knew he couldn't understand her muffled words.

"You are the girl I planned to marry, Bella. But Jack ruined all of that, so I had to take matters into my own hands." Mason struck a rock with his boot, the chipping sound grating on her nerves.

"So what I've done is taken his wife. I will finally have my revenge on Jack. This time in order to get you back, your dear husband will have to pay me a very generous amount."

"Get comfortable Bella, this will likely be a very long night for you." Mason started to walk away, before he turned. "You won't be rescued by Jack until he gives me the money I deserve. Sweet dreams Bella."

As the echo of Mason's boots disappeared in the distance, a chilling, tingly, sweaty kind of fear took hold of her.

She tried to take a deep breath, but the gag tied to her mouth only let in about half the air she needed.

A metallic taste flooded her mouth as terror rushed through her pores in a sweat that reeked of fear.

Memories of the kidnapping years ago started a fear of

enclosed spaces inside her mind. Right now that fear was growing and threatened to overpower all rational thought.

Mentally Bella pushed away the terror that filled every cell of her being. A sharp pain gnawed between Bella's eyes at her predicament.

Her hands and feet grew cold and stiff and she moved them as much as she could. She had no idea where she was.

Only a tiny light peeked through what must have been a gap in the cave's wall, near the ceiling. She watched it for a long while, the darkness hovering, watching.

A different kind of fear than Bella had ever known grabbed hold: a chilling, tingly, clammy kind of fear. It's cold tendrils wrapped around her ankles and crept up her spine to the back of her neck.

Bella wanted to run, but the ropes were knotted tight around her ankles. She screamed but to her own ears the sound didn't reach much farther than the gag around her mouth.

How long before someone realized she was missing? Would they be able to find her hidden in the darkness?

Bella remembered her husband's warm kisses. She realized that she loved him more than anything else in her life.

Awareness grew inside her at that moment.

Her greatest desire to be independent and in control — wasn't as important as what she really needed… which was to be loved by her husband. She needed to be loved by Jack -- the one man she loved with all her heart.

In this moment, she realized that she would willingly

give up her independence to live everyday with the man she loved.

Right now, Jack was mad at her, but she had confidence Jack would do everything he could to rescue her once again.

Jack, please find me quickly.

CHAPTER SIXTEEN

Jack

JACK HIT the pickaxe against the brittle rock on the silver mine's wall. Anger and guilt both gnawed at him.

He shouldn't have been so hard on Bella. He'd spoken to her in anger, frustrated that his wife had gone behind his back and managed to get into the one room he'd told her not to enter.

That room was the place that held his deepest pain, failures and secrets. That was the one room he went into regularly to remind himself of his failures. It was a place to mourn what was lost and a continual reminder of the costly price of mistakes.

It was a constant reminder of his errors in judgement

— such as giving his heart to a woman or longing for a son of his own — ensuring he wouldn't repeat them.

Problem was, his heart was at war with his logical mind.

Already he was falling for Bella.

Which was why in the conservatory the other night, he'd done his best to push her away.

But the more he stayed away from her, the more he longed for her.

Seeing her standing before him today with her brown eyes made larger against her pale face, had niggled at his conscience.

After throwing his weight behind the force of the pickaxe a couple more times, he leaned it against the hard dirt wall.

He hurried toward the mine's entrance. It was time to go back home and apologize to his wife.

Mike was talking to one of the workers, when he saw Jack. "How's it going?" His foreman hurried to keep up with Jack.

"Still haven't struck gold yet, so I'll keep trying." Jack reached his ATV and turned to Mike. "On my way home. I'll see you tomorrow."

With a quick wave at Mike, Jack hurried home.

As he stepped inside the entryway of his home, he hung up his jacket and went to shower and change. Only then, did he look for Bella.

Knocking on her bedroom door, he didn't receive any answer, so he opened the door. Everything was neat and tidy, but his wife was absent.

Sure she must be in her office, he hurried down the

hallway and opened the door to Bella's office, only to find it empty.

He spotted Ben in the Library and hurried over. "Did Bella leave? I can't seem to find her anywhere in this house."

"But sir, I thought she was with you." Ben's eyes widened with worry.

Fear snaked up like a coil in Jack's belly. "Well she did come to see me at the mine, but then I assumed she went straight home."

"Well, that's the thing, sir. I don't think she returned home." Ben's expression was a mixture of surprise and confusion. "I'll ask Mrs. Potter, but I don't think either of us have seen her since she left early this morning."

Jack's brow puckered in worry at Ben's words. "What? Where could she be then?"

"I'll ask Mrs. Potter. We'll search until we find her, sir."

The loud ringing of Jack's cell phone interrupted their conversation. "This is Bella, now."

"Hi Bella." Jack immediately heard a low male voice, laughing in the background.

Anger surged out of him. "Who is this? And how did you get my wife's cell phone?"

"Jack, you don't recognize me? This is Mason." Another bout of mocking laughter followed. "I have your wife's cell phone, because I took it from her."

"Where is she? I demand to speak to her now!" Jack paced the room, gripping the phone tighter, his knuckles turning white.

"Sorry, I can't do that, Jack. The deal is that in order

for you to see your wife again, you'll have to pay me twenty million dollars."

Jack couldn't believe what he was hearing. "Why are you doing this, Mason?"

Another sarcastic chuckle was heard at the other end of the phone line. "Because Jack, you stole the woman I was going to marry. You took what I wanted most. So now I'm going to hit you where it'll hurt the most."

Jack expelled an angry breath. "Don't do this Mason. This won't end well for you."

"*Au contraire.* I think this will end very well for me." More mocking laughter was heard on the other end of the phone line. "But, you Jack are going down. Get the money to me by noon tomorrow. I'll call you again to tell you the location."

"Where do you have Bella, Mason?" Jack was desperate to know.

Mason's voice was low and menacing. "I have her hidden in the place of her worst fears… you'll never find her. After you get me the money, I'll tell you where she is."

The phone clicked off.

Jack looked up to see Ben standing by the Library door. "You heard that?"

"Yes, what are you going to do?"

I'm going to find her, if I have to search all night long." Jack hurried to the front entrance, slipping his jacket on. He paused and turned to Ben. "There was one thing Mason said which seemed a little strange."

Ben raised one eyebrow in question. "What's that?"

"He said he hid Bella in the place of her worst fears."

Jack paced around the front entrance, as he thought it through.

"That's got to be someplace where she'll feel trapped then."

"Yes, and dark." A sudden awareness came to Jack. "Of course… the silver mine. We've got to hurry."

Ben slipped on his jacket and shoes and hurried after Jack as they went out the door. Brahms wagged his tail and jumped in the truck beside them.

Jack started his truck and they drove along the well-used trail to Grand's mine.

"I've got a blanket and extra flashlights, sir."

"Good, we'll need them." Jack turned on the light attached to his miner's helmet and walked inside the deep cave. Dark clouds gathered in the sky above, making the cave even darker than usual.

The men had gone home and it was silent as they hurried forward.

Three different tunnels appeared, but Jack knew the mine well as he remembered all the times he'd been explored the tunnels as a boy with his great-grandfather.

"Which one do we take?" Ben's whisper sounded loud in the stillness.

"The third tunnel on the right." He knew the other two well, but it was this third tunnel that led to the deepest caverns and most treacherous part of the mine.

Brahms trotted along with them and they walked for a really long time, before they came to a yawning cavern. This was a place where there were needle-like rocks hanging down from the ceiling and sticking up from the ground.

"Watch your step. Easy to fall on these." Jack spoke as he shone the flashlight in his hand to all the nooks and crannies of the cave.

Suddenly, Brahms leapt forward, twisting his way toward a large rock in the far corner.

Jack followed his dog hope rising in his chest. "Bella?"

He stepped around jagged rock formations and almost tripped in his hurry to reach his wife. A low moan reached his ears as he neared a large rock.

Jack searched around until he saw his wife. Brahms was licking her face. She was gagged, her hands and feet tied tight.

Clutching her shoulders with both hands, he squatted looking at the bruises and cuts on her neck, arms and face.

Jack's anger felt like a large fist stuck in his throat that he couldn't get rid of.

"Oh sweetheart. What did that monster do to you?" With shaky hands, Jack untied the gag around Bella's mouth and then just as quickly cut off the ropes that bound her hands and feet.

He pulled out the handkerchief he held in his pocket and dabbed lightly at the cuts on her face, neck and hands.

Bella grabbed onto his hands.

Lifting her in his arms, he kissed her quickly, breathing her in.

"You're here, Jack." Bella twisted and moaned, her eyes opened looking half dazed.

Jack picked her up, holding her in his arms. "Of course I'm here darling. It's time to get you home."

"Not so fast, Jack." A low and sinister voice spoke from behind them.

Jack turned just in time to see Mason charging from behind.

Dropping Bella to her feet, he moved her behind him to protect her.

Mason threw his fist into Jack's stomach. Jack punched him back and lost his balance.

Throwing a punch at Jack's chin, Mason pushed him backwards. From the light on his helmet, Jack could see they were standing near the edge of a rocky cliff with a deep cavern below.

Jack shifted, but Mason shoved him again and Jack lost his balance and slipped so he was clinging to rock in order not to fall into the crevice below.

Mason's menacing chuckle reverberated off the dirt walls. "You weren't supposed to find her, but you couldn't help yourself could you?" Jack's attacker stepped closer and stepped on his right hand. Pain arched through his hand, causing him to almost lose his grip.

Out of the corner of his eye, Jack saw Bella stand up and with a commanding voice spoke to his dog. "Brahms, attack."

Brahms ran toward Mason, his large paws hitting him in the chest. He landed on his back, with Brahms teeth bared, growling at Mason, daring him to make a wrong move.

Bella hurried over to Jack and grabbed his hands, helping him stand on solid ground once more.

"Thank you, my love." Jack kissed her on the lips.

Suddenly Ben walked into the cavern with three police officers behind him.

Two of the police officers walked toward Mason. Jack

called off his dog as one officer held him down while the other officer placed handcuffs on his wrists.

"I'm glad you called earlier Jack. It was just as you suspected. This man followed you into the mine to do you harm." One of the police officers held up a loaded gun and a pack of explosives. "Here's the proof."

"That's not all the evidence there is to arrest Mason, officers." Bella spoke up. "I think you'll be interested in documents hidden in Mason's office at the town office that reveal a shady and unethical plan for funding the Wolffe brothers and Senator Wolffe's re-election. You'll find re-allocation of funds from donations given to a campaign and transferring those funds to a black market alias name that is really a front for human trafficking. This is not only unethical but also illegal."

Bella paused. "You'll also find the documents that were stolen out of Senator Carver's office. Ask Mason's secretary Tiffany, about that. And I think you'll also be interested in seeing the photos and names of men who are experts in chemicals and homemade bombs as well as a schedule of places and times these are set to go off. Seems like they were planning this for months."

The police officer beside them raised an eyebrow and let out a low whistle.

"Bella, how dare you go through my private papers!" Mason stepped toward Bella his expression livid, but the officer held him tight.

"Well, it looks like we'll be getting a search warrant. Thanks Jack and Bella." They police officer shook their hands.

Mason glared at Jack and Bella a wild-eyed expression face. "This isn't over yet."

"Yes, I believe it is Mason." Jack lifted Bella once more into his arms and followed Ben toward the tunnel entrance.

Pausing, he looked back once more at Mason and spoke to the police officers. "He's all yours gentlemen."

With Ben leading the way, Jack followed carrying Bella in his arms. He was eager to get his wife home.

As soon as they arrived home, Ben took care of Brahms and Jack carried Bella to her bedroom. After calling for Nurse Marmie, she came quickly. Jack left the room while the nurse took care of his wife's many cuts and bruises.

Bella lay quietly on her bed when Jack returned. He sat down on one corner, staring at her for a long time, knots of fear still angling their way up from his belly to his throat.

"Bella." Jack ground out her name as though in torment and reached for his wife, hauling her into his arms with the force of his need.

All the pent up fears and worries suddenly came crashing down on Jack. "I thought I'd lost you. I nearly went mad with fear. I can't bear to go through that again."

"Does that mean you forgive me for going against your wishes and opening the door to your secret room?" Bella's large brown eyes were doe-like and solemn.

"Of course I forgive you." Jack swallowed back the emotion that threatened to consume him. He pulled her onto his lap, raining kisses on her eyelids and cheeks. "I finally realized today when I nearly lost you, how much you mean to me."

His chest heaved and Jack closed his eyes trying to shut out the vivid images of seeing her bound and gagged in the cave. Jack's hands stroked her hair and he released jagged breaths.

"Heaven help me Bella, but once I realized Mason held you hostage at the mine, I couldn't get to you fast enough."

He stared at her, expelling a breath, shutting his eyes for a brief moment.

❧

"Jack," Bella whispered, her mouth so close to his that their breath melded together as one. "I'm here now. I'm safe. You saved me."

She reached a hand up and touched his cheek, peering into her husband's haunted eyes.

He nodded but his eyes still seemed pained, refusing to leave her face. Then ever so slowly, almost as if he expected her to pull away, Jack moved his lips closer to hers. "I can't stand the thought of losing you. I'd rather die myself."

Bella turned her face to accept his kiss, unable to deny him anything.

He tangled shaky hands in her thick brown hair, holding her captive, his lips ravaging hers with an intensity that sent her senses reeling. Nothing mattered in this moment, except the warmth of her husband's touch. A fierce tenderness rose up on the inside as Bella fervently fed his need.

Jack's heartfelt whisper caused her to come undone. "My sweet Bella, I can't lose you."

"You won't. I'm here… I'm here." Her body molded to her husband's and she offered her lips up to his loving mastery. Over and over he kissed her, until she was breathless.

Bella reached up, her arms encircling his neck drawing him closer.

It was this devotion that she had longed for almost from the start. Her heart basked in the realization that he needed her.

Jack pulled his mouth from hers with a low moan as if unwilling to part from her for one moment. His strong arms cradled her close to his chest and she could hear the rapid beating of his heart. A deep sense of happiness and contentment filled her.

Her husband continued to stroke her hair and Bella snuggled closer to his heart.

She adored being held in Jack's arms and was filled with wonderful sensations from each of his kisses.

Yet, there was something even more powerful about the tender way he held her now. Today, she sensed a deeper connection to Jack, almost like they had bonded their spirits in a way they hadn't before.

Her husband had told her that he'd become attached to her, but it was only now that she'd finally believed him. Bella swallowed back the emotion that threatened to consume her.

They sat together in silence for a long time, and Bella cherished this time of closeness with her husband.

"I'm sorry for how I've pushed you away for so long." Jack's gruff whisper broke through the stillness of the moment. "I told you about losing my wife and son in that car accident, but I've finally realized all that pain and heartache made me too afraid to love another. A big part of that pain has been from my fear of failing and losing the woman I love again."

Bella felt the weight of Jack's sorrow in his words.

She remembered the words of Jack's Grandmom. *All of my grandson's pain has made him too afraid to love again. He's been too afraid of trusting another woman and misreading her motives. He's afraid of being hurt, so he pushes people away before he can be hurt by them. That's why I'm so glad he has you by his side to show him how to trust again. He has you by his side to show him how to love again.*

"It's okay, Jack." Bella tightened her grip around his waist, aware of how difficult it must be for him to speak of his wife and son.

Her husband's body tensed, "No it's not okay, Bella. Don't you see? I don't want to hide from love. But, I failed to truly love and protect Elin and our son the way they needed me to. What if I fail you — I couldn't stand it if I lost you too."

"It wasn't your fault that Elin decided to leave you. It wasn't your fault that your wife and unborn son passed away in that accident." Bella moved back a little ways to look into Jack's eyes, her own cloudy with unshed tears.

"But it was. I was the one responsible for them both." Jack pressed his eyes shut, a harsh groan falling from his lips. "For years, the weight of their deaths has all but crushed me. I'm terrified that somehow I'll repeat the same mistakes with you, because I love you so much that it scares me to live day after day in a world without you in it."

He expelled a labored breath. "Which is why I've decided to give up hiding away in fear. I want to spend a lifetime learning how to love you, Bella."

A single tear slipped down her cheek. He reached over and with gentle fingers wiped away her tears.

She turned to look into her husband's eyes.

"You love me?"

"I have for weeks. I think I fell in love with you at that dinner party weeks ago. And it's also why I've been so bad-tempered all these weeks as I've tried my best to push you away and ignore these feelings." He ran a shaky hand through his hair and grimaced. "I'm sorry for that."

Bella revelled in hearing her husband's words of love. "I forgive you. I love you too with all my heart."

Jack pulled her closer and kissed her briefly. "I've been drawn to you from the first. You're a woman who is warm, gentle and kind. Someone who also happens to be selfless, beautiful and very... desirable." Jack faltered on the last word, as his eyes darkened and moved down to her lips.

She swallowed back emotion at his words, forcing herself to meet his gaze.

He whispered words mingled close to her lips. "I want to kiss you so badly right now, but first I need to know something."

"What?"

"When we first married, we agreed this was a fake marriage that would benefit us both. But it seems we've fallen in love." Jack leaned his forehead against hers, his eyes squeezing shut, pausing for a moment. "Do you think you would mind being married for real to a beast like me?"

Bella let out the breath she'd been holding and a shaky smile formed on her lips.

Jack's fierce love for her coupled with his need to have her as his forever wife, was the most compelling reason to make this marriage real. "Jack, you're not a beast… not to me. You've saved me, you've trusted me with the most vulnerable part of yourself and you've honored me with your love. More than anything, I would be proud to be your wife in every way."

She shivered with anticipation at the tender passion she saw in his eyes.

Softly she whispered. "Love me, Jack."

Her husband's lips touched her own with a sweet reckless abandon. Jack's arms tightened around her and he rolled her so she was lying on her back. His hands reached up to cradle her face, dark hazel eyes searching hers a hesitation in his movements.

Bella leaned up and brushed her lips against his, her kisses saying much more than words ever could.

Jack groaned unable to wait a second longer, he folded her in his arms, kissing her with the hunger of a starved man. "Bella, my beautiful wife. You've changed my life."

Then her husband kissed her again, leaving her with no doubt, that both their love and marriage was wonderfully real.

CHAPTER SEVENTEEN

N̄ine months later...

"Wᴇ'ʀᴇ ᴛʀɪʟʟᴇᴅ to have so many people from Paradise Lake join us for the Grand Opening of the Rose Adventure Park." Mayor Rainey's sing-song voice rang out over the large crowd.

"As many of you are aware, there were people who created problems in their efforts to hinder the building of this Adventure Park. We're happy to say that those responsible for all the trouble have been stopped. The police have taken appropriate action to see justice done."

The Mayor waited until the cheering stopped before continuing, "Once again, I want to apologize to Jack and Bella Stevenson. We're so happy you pushed forward to build this very beautiful Adventure Park in spite of all the obstacles in your way. It's an exciting day for all of us in

Paradise Lake. Congratulations." Mayor Rainey smiled and shook hands with Jack and Bella who stepped behind the podium.

Jack surveyed the crowd for a moment in silence. From his vantage point behind the podium, Jack could see the newly finished pink princess castle, a large mountain Rollercoaster and many other fun rides. He was surprised to see so many of the townsfolk who had come here today.

Frankly, he was bewildered at the show of support, especially since so many people in Paradise Lake didn't seem to like him very much. However that dislike had changed to acceptance in the weeks since he'd married Bella.

With Bella as his wife, instead of seeing him as a beast, the townsfolk began to look at him in a better light. The truth was, since his marriage to Bella, he'd started to see himself differently… like a man no longer consumed with the guilt and pain of his past.

Bella's belief in him along with her unconditional acceptance and love had changed him.

He looked over at his beautiful wife still amazed she was truly his.

Jack accepted the microphone from Mayer Rainey and with a nod said, "Thanks Mayor. We are thrilled that this project is complete. As you can tell from the variety of rides and buildings behind you, this has been a huge task to complete in the last nine months, but we did it. Our goal was to finish this adventure park before the birth of our son and it looks like we made it just in time."

Turning toward his wife, Jack placed a gentle hand on

her large belly. Bella looked up at him with a big smile on her face and placed her hand over his.

He turned back to speak to the crowd, "There are so many people who helped us get this finished and who we want to thank. First, we want to say thanks to the Paradise Lake town and town council for supporting us in this venture. We're grateful for your belief in this project."

Jack searched the crowd to find their team. "Second, Bella and I would like to thank Stevenson Creative Works design team and many others for working so many over-time hours so we could get this done on time. Third, we'd like to say a big thank you to our friends and family for your encouragement and understanding when we had to say no to different invitations due to a crazy schedule."

His gaze searched the crowd to see his mom, grand-parents and brothers along with Elle and baby Daniel all sitting together in the front row. Not far from them sat Bella's Dad, his new wife Marmie and Bella's aunt Maisie. Each of them wore big smiles on their faces.

He turned and slipped his arm around Bella, kissing her on the cheek. "Last, but definitely not least, I want to express my most heartfelt thanks to my beautiful wife."

Bella's upturned face glowed beside him. "She has encouraged and believed in me every step of the way. In every way possible, I have felt her acceptance and love. Together we have decided to donate the proceeds of this first opening day, to the Stevenson BeSafe Foundation which is dedicated to helping victims of human traf-ficking."

Jack walked with Bella toward the ceremonial ribbon. Mayor Rainey handed Jack the scissors, and as he held them in his hand he paused, swallowing back emotion. "I've decided to make a slight change to the name of this Adventure Park, in recognition of the amazing woman who has changed my world. I give you the *Bella Rose Adventure Park.*"

Jack cut the ribbon, and the crowd cheered.

He peered over at his wife, wondering how she'd take the announcement.

Her big brown eyes widened and filled with moisture. "Thank you, Jack. I can't believe you named this Adventure Park after me." The crowd cheered and Bella stood on her tiptoes to kiss him. "I love you."

"And I love you." Jack kissed her quickly and then looked back out at the crowd. "Enjoy the rides, everyone." Jack waved at the people who cheered once more before moving away to explore the new adventure park.

Jack slid his arms around his wife's protruding belly pulling her close, wanting more of her kisses. She pulled back, her cheeks blossoming into that sweet pink color he loved so much.

"You mean the world to me Bella. Its just one small way that I can show you how much I love you." Jack leaned down to kiss her again.

Without warning his wife gasped and clutched a hand to her swollen belly.

❦

"I think my waters have broke." Bella could feel heat crawling up her neck to her cheeks.

Her husband's brow puckered with worry as he

noticed her brown eyes growing wider. "You're in labor, right now?" Jack's normally calm features were replaced by a look of sheer panic.

Bella only nodded and groaned as a wave of pain wrapped its way around her middle. The initial shock and embarrassment at finding herself in this predicament, was quickly replaced by excitement of their soon-to-be born son.

Jack slipped his arm around her and she leaned on him for support.

Aunt Maisie walked toward them. "Bella, is something wrong?"

Bella looked over at her aunt with a shaky smile. "It seems it's time for our baby to be born."

"Oh heavens." Her aunt seemed to be beside herself.

"Aunt Maisie it's okay. Thousands of women have children everyday. But, I think we'll be going to the Hospital now."

"Yes, we're off to the Hospital. Maisie could you let the others in the family know where we've gone?"

"Oh, of course my dears. We'll meet you there." Aunt Maisie fluttered away to talk to Bella's Dad.

Bella focused on breathing through each contraction. Jack had insisted they take the childbirth classes together so they had a better idea of what to expect during labor and afterwards. She hadn't wanted to go, but at this moment she was grateful for what she'd learned.

Her husband picked her up in his strong arms and carried her to his waiting truck.

"Jack, what are you doing?" Bella slipped her arm around his neck.

"Getting you to the Hospital quickly, my love." Jack kissed her on the cheek as he gently set her down on the truck's cushioned seat.

She sighed. For once happy about her husband's take-charge ways.

They got to the Hospital in record time. Jack slipped his arms around her and carried her inside.

Before long she was whisked away and given a room.

Jack stayed by her side, giving her ice cubes to chew on in between labor pains.

It didn't take long before the nurse examined her a second time and called for the Doctor. "Looks like this baby is eager to arrive." The doctor began to coach her to push between contractions.

Jack held her hand and whispered in her ear. "Our son is almost here, Bella. One more push. You can do this."

Bella gave a final push and the baby slipped out into the Doctor's waiting hands. After the doctor cut the cord and double-checked that the baby was breathing well, she wrapped him in a warm blanket and placed his tiny body in Bella's waiting arms.

"Our son. He's beautiful." She kissed the top of his head and peered over at Jack.

A look of amazed wonder was on Jack's face as he stared at his son.

"Thank you Bella for the incredible gift of our son." Jack kissed her tenderly. A single tear escaped and ran down her husband's cheek. She kissed it away.

"Should we name him after your great-grandfather?" Bella kissed the the tiny infant's forehead before handing him to Jack.

Jack carefully embraced his son, his hands shaking slightly. "Walker Stevenson?" Jack gaze covered the top of his tiny son's head all the way to his tiny toes.

Bella nodded and her eyes sparkled at her husband's scrutiny of their new son.

"Why don't we name him after Grand and your dad? Walker Dunlin Stevenson sounds about right, don't you think?" Jack's gaze shifted over to her, a wobbly smile softening his usual pirate look.

"It's perfect. And thanks for thinking of my dad. He'll be as proud as a peacock." Bella was about to say more, when Eliza Stevenson poked her head in the door.

"Can we come in yet? I'm eager to meet my grandson."

"Of course mom." Bella loved to see Jack's smile which was as wide and proud as she'd ever seen it. His mom and grandparents each took turns holding their new grandson. Dunlin, Marmie and aunt Maisie followed close behind along with Adam, Elle, baby Daniel and Jack's four brothers.

Dunlin beamed a smile as heard his grandson's name. "Well, I'm honored. Beauty, he's a son to be proud of."

"Thanks Dad. Now, you can begin to make memories with him like you did with me."

"Aye, Lassie. It's happy and proud I am to do it." Dunlin held his first grandson close to his heart.

That afternoon was spent with their families, admiring the newest Stevenson.

A few days later Jack brought Bella and their baby boy home.

The Stevenson family wanted to have a party for Jack and Bella and the new addition to their family.

"I have a gift I want to give you before we join the family." Jack held his son with one hand and embraced his wife close to his side with the other.

They walked down the hallway toward their rooms, and Jack stopped by the door to the secret room. "I've made a few changes." The corners of his mouth turned up and he opened the door. "What do you think?"

Bella eyes widened and she smiled at the changes.

The walls had been stripped bare of the haunting pictures that used to hang there and were repainted in beautiful rainbow colors. On the biggest wall was a hand painted mural of Noah's Ark with cute animals everywhere.

A new rocking chair was in one corner and a new baby crib was in the other with a large archway that separated the baby room and the master bedroom.

Bella's gaze circled the room.

Gone were the harsh reminders of Jack's painful past. The walls were fresh and clean almost like a forgiveness and redemption of sorts.

This room of secrets had been transformed into a soft haven scattered with rainbows of promise.

Her gaze shifted to look outside the large window. Bella put her hand to her mouth in surprise, when she saw a double rainbow in the sky. "I think it's beautiful Jack. It's a new beginning for us." Bella's swallowed back tears of happiness. Her eyes latched onto his, not letting go.

"I agree." Jack's gaze studied her features and his lips formed a smile.

He looked at his son and back at her. "I never thought I'd have another chance. I am incredibly grateful that you agreed to be my real wife. You are all my dreams come true."

He pulled her closer, his gaze holding hers. "I want you and I to make a home together with our baby boy and with as many children as you want. I want our family to be happy and whole. I want everything but mostly, Bella Rose Stevenson, I want you to know how much you are loved." He paused to let his declaration sink in. "I love you more than I've ever loved a woman before. You are my life."

Tears streamed down Bella's cheeks and she lifted her hands up to cup his face, holding him steady. "You don't ever do anything by halves, do you?"

"I guess not. But, I pushed you away far too long, Bella. I pushed away your love. I regret that it took almost losing you forever to make me understand just what we were — what you mean to me. I was almost too late." Jack's voice cracked and she could see regret in his eyes.

"No, not too late Jack. Right on time." Bella stood on tiptoe to touch her lips to his.

He pulled her close, settling his lips on hers.

His hand gripped her tighter and he deepened the kiss. Pulling back he stared into her eyes.

"I'll love you forever, Bella Rose Stevenson." Jack's declaration was something she would never tire of hearing.

"I love you too, Jack Walker Stevenson... forever."

GABE

GABE STEVENSON LOOKED around the great room of his brother Jack's home, happy to be back with his family again.

As he watched his Granddad play checkers with Jack, his brothers arm wrestling each other and his GrandMom and Mom holding little Daniel and baby Walker, warmth flooded him.

His brother's wives, Elle and Bella, sipped tea while talking and laughing together.

It made him long for more of the love of family. It made him long for love.

"Hey Gabe." Jack handed him a coffee and motioned for him to follow. "Let's go outside. It's beautiful outside after the rain." They walked out onto the large deck that overlooked his massive backyard.

"I'm surprised to see you. Why are you still here? Usually every few weeks you're flying out to speak at a conference or a TV interview or something similar." They sunk down onto the cushioned chairs on the deck that overlooked Jack and Bella's beautiful rose garden.

Taking a sip of his coffee Gabe looked at his brother. "I was able to get back just in time for the Grand Opening of the *Bella Rose Adventure Park* and of course now that your silver mine is steadily producing silver along with a few veins of gold, I wanted to celebrate your success."

"Thanks for that Gabe. That means the world to me and Bella."

Raising his cup towards Jack, he smiled. "Of course. And to answer your question, my plan for the next six weeks is to have time out of the spotlight for a while. Time to simply breathe."

"I can understand that. Since you've become so famous, that's probably more difficult than ever."

Gabe shifted in his seat, tossing his brother a rueful smile. For him it was always a little uncomfortable when his family talked about how well known he was. He knew they were just teasing, but he sometimes envied the fact that his brothers could go places without a bunch of people taking pictures of them.

That's why he loved coming home. Being near his family was a safe place for him where he could simply be himself.

That normal life is what he realized he'd been yearning for.

"It is. I'm trying to figure out how I can escape the public eye for a few weeks. So far, I've come up with nothing." Gabe set down his cup, stood to his feet and walked toward the railing.

Jack followed. "There just might be a way, that is if you don't mind being without the usual conveniences."

"That would be great. What are you thinking?"

"Well, Great-Grandfather did give you Walker's Island in his will. That old hunting lodge on the property is sitting there empty and might be ideal right about now."

Gabe nodded, surprised he didn't think of that himself.

"Didn't Grand arrange for three sisters and their niece to live on a corner of that Island?"

"Yes. He said those sisters had saved his life when he was young, and because of that he promised them they could have ten acres on a corner of that forested Island where they could live rent-free for the rest of their lives." The reminder of Grand's will requirement, that all his great-grandsons marry by their twenty-seventh birthday made him aware that the deadline was drawing closer.

"I seem to remember something like that." Gabe sighed. Well, that put a kink in his plans. He wanted to have solitude. Maybe he'd go anyway. Even with the four women living in a cabin on the corner of Grand's Island, most of the time he'd have peace and quiet if he stayed at the hunting lodge. He needed to do this. "All right. I'll do it. I'll go there tomorrow."

"Well good, I'm glad that's settled. A few weeks at Grand's hunting lodge, might be just what you need." Jack grinned and patted him on the back. "Maybe you can take this time to think about the woman you want to marry."

Gabe peered over at his brother, a grimace hovering over his lips. "Well, so far all the women I've dated are interested in only two things: my connections, or my money. They don't see me as an ordinary man and they certainly don't see the real me."

He shook his head slightly. "I'm not convinced there is a woman out there who will."

"Oh ye of little faith." Jack chuckled. "She's out there, I'm sure of it little brother. And maybe like me, you'll suddenly find the woman you'll fall in love with in the place you least expect it… right under your nose." Jack bumped up against Gabe's shoulder and grinned.

Well, Jack might have found the woman who was the love of his life, but he wasn't convinced it would happen for him.

Women that dated him so far wanted the glamour he could give them, his track record proved that. He didn't believe there was a woman out there who would love him for who he was instead of for who they wanted him to be.

He needed a woman who was smart, but someone who could also laugh at herself. He needed a woman who didn't mind living in the quiet, but who could also handle the spotlight. He needed a woman who would give him the freedom to be himself and love him for who he was.

Where in the world would he find this jewel of a woman?

No, Gabe couldn't see himself finding a woman like that anywhere. He peered up at the darkening clouds that hinted at a coming storm.

Maybe finding real love simply wasn't possible for a man like him.

***

S TART READING GABE'S STORY IN "T HE B ILLIONAIRE'S M ARRIAGE P ROMISE" TODAY!

Billionaire Gabe Stevenson is a well known and loved by millions.

He's got it all, except the love of a woman who sees him and loves him for who he really is.

Rory has grown up hidden from the world on a forested Island with her three aunts. She writes about love in her bestselling romance novels, but has never experienced true love for herself.

When Gabe needs a break from his grueling schedule he returns to the solitude of his great-grandfather's Island Hunting Lodge only to find an innocent sleeping beauty disrupting his peace and quiet.

He's determined to stay away from Rory, but when he discovers the superstitions of the Island and that someone has gone to great lengths to make these fears seem real, Gabe insists Rory stay by his side to protect her.

Will being forced together tear Gabe and Rory apart or will it instead throw them towards true love?

ABOUT THE AUTHOR

Melody Archer lives in Alberta with her husband and their four young adults.

Recently, her oldest son married and their family has been enjoying getting to know their oldest son's wife from Brazil ~ their new daughter-in-love. :)

She loves new and classic romantic movies, green smoothies and going on adventures with her family.

Melody would love to connect with you :)

facebook.com/melodyarcherauthor
instagram.com/melodyarcherauthor
bookbub.com/profile/melody-archer
pinterest.com/melodyarcherauthor

ACKNOWLEDGMENTS

Thank you to all the wonderful people who helped me with this book.

To my cover designer, Wilette from Red Leaf Book Design, thank you for designing this gorgeous book cover.

Thank you also, to my proofreader Cathy who patiently read through each chapter, helping me make this story so much better.

A big thanks to all my wonderful Advanced Readers (my ARC reading team), who faithfully read and left reviews of this book.

Lastly, a huge thanks to three of my young adult children who read through the manuscript, giving me all kinds of great suggestions on how to make this a better story.

Thank you everyone. I really appreciate you!:)

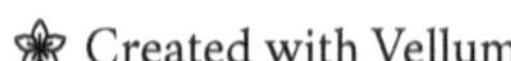 Created with Vellum